# FULL MOONS AND VAMPIRES
## A DEATHLESS LOVE NOVELLA

### ZORA FOX

# WELCOME TO THE EIGHT REALMS

A land of gods and goddesses—a savage, beautiful collection of islands in the Corae Sea. The stories here are violent, with explicit sexual content not intended for anyone under 18. These books about deathless love feature dark, often twisted romances. Enter at your own risk.

ZENIA

Ruled by Thenios, God-King of lightning

## APHRISO

Ruled by Cytherea, goddess of pleasure

## ERISET

Contested land, ruled by Ares and Bellona, god and goddess of war

## MENOS

Ruled by Scira, goddess of wisdom

## NALIA

Ruled by Basileus, god of the ocean

## HYPERION

Ruled by Lox, god of the sun

## KANTHAROS

Ruled by Vesta, goddess of hearth and home

## FAR REALM

Ruled by Hades, god of the dead

Content warnings for this story of deathless love: explicit sex (including group scenes), bondage, blood, language

# JUNIPER

"Do you believe in perfect mates?"

"No."

I crunched another walnut, frowning. "You don't? I read today that all vampires believe in one true soulmate."

Luca eyed me with amused suspicion. He folded his black wings, adjusting his reading position in the velvet chair. "And I heard that all fauns live in the forest. We're not all the same, Juniper."

"I wasn't saying you're all the same." My Hingat accent came out stronger in my frustration.

"And you've known that fact for ages. Before you read it today for the Assembly."

I pursed my lips in a little smile. He caught me. "Well, yes."

"So why are you bringing it up now?" He set down the book he was reading—*Salts and Spice*—and beckoned me onto his lap.

I couldn't resist. Not with that smooth voice and those

deep-set eyes. The slightest movement in them conveyed profound depth and emotion. A crinkle in the corners meant laughter. The barest downturn of his dark eyebrows meant deep hurt. An unflinching, sparkling stare meant he wanted my clothes off.

Settling onto his strong thighs, I saw a hint of that look. "You've never mentioned it," I replied.

"That vampires believe in perfect mates? Is that something you would talk about all the time?"

He kept skirting around an answer. Must have been the full moon coming up next week. That always put him on edge.

I had to be careful talking about his vampire heritage. He kept parts of his culture secret from me, which drove me mad. I shouldn't have held it against him—there were parts of my upbringing as a faun that I didn't talk about—but it stoked my curiosity to a frenzy.

Plus, not everyone thought I was smart to fall for a vampire. Flings happened, but not love. Not with a faun. I didn't want to be seen as prey, as young, as naïve by people who saw us together. Pitying looks weren't uncommon. They made me grind my molars. Was it so strange that we could be in love?

Luca caressed the place below my knee where my skin gave way to soft brown fur. His pale fingers felt cool.

"I would talk about it with you," I insisted. Maybe I was pushing too much, but he'd said *no*. "I wouldn't leave you to do your own research when an expert lived right here." I tapped him on the nose.

His shoulders eased and eyes softened. "Fair enough. Most

vampires believe in perfect mates. I'm just not one of them. Besides," he added silkily, "you like doing research."

Lamplight traced his high pale cheekbones and shadowed his black hair. The way he gazed at me, eyes trailing down my freckled skin, made me squeeze my legs together. The movement made him look down. His jaw flexed, expression darkening, and he lightly shook out one wing.

"Are you uncomfortable?" I asked, pulling away to stand up. Maybe the high back of the chair had cramped his wings. I'd look for a new one soon. "We can move."

Luca laughed, the ice from a moment ago shattering. "Holding you? No, I'm not uncomfortable." Moonlight streamed through the window, adding ghostly blue to the lamplight. He fished in his pocket and pulled out a salt bead. The quick flash of his fangs caught the light as he threw it in his mouth and sucked. "Most ways."

He needed more salt beads with the full moon coming. They replaced his craving for blood. By now, I associated the taste of salt with Luca's lips.

"You're always wondering if I'm uncomfortable, if I need something," he said, drawing me back onto his lap. "You should think more about yourself." His arms circled my waist, but there was a slight stiffness to his limbs that said he was trying to avoid touching my thigh—the spot where he'd left a nasty bruise last month, right before he traveled home for a couple days. He felt so bad about that when he returned that I was just glad he was holding me like this again.

"I feel like I'm always thinking about myself and the Assembly."

"As you should." His voice became a seductive murmur.

"My leader of gods and goddesses..." He nuzzled his nose into the crook of my neck.

My skin warmed. "Hardly," I laughed. Luca and I were both mortal, but I led the research and city development team in the Assembly building, a huge achievement for a faun. And I had plans for even bigger titles.

He released a cool breath and backed away enough to face me. Amusement and even regret chased each other over his face. His pupils were still blown black. "I'm sorry, Juniper."

"For wh—"

"Ask a different question. I promise I'll answer."

I linked my fingers together. "Like you did when I asked you about my outfit for the last Assembly Ball?"

He rolled his eyes, smirking. "You looked stunning."

"I had a big sauce stain on my lap!"

"I didn't notice."

"How could you not notice? When Glaucus pointed it out, I was mortified. I'm trying to get promoted there, you know."

That infuriating half-smile I loved so much hadn't left his face. I scrunched up my nose in return.

"I failed you," Luca said without a scrap of remorse. His finger wandered up to trace my breast, then my cheek. "I was too distracted."

"Unacceptable."

"Would you like me to make you something less saucy before the next event?"

I laughed. "Less saucy?"

"That's what I said." He drew closer. Luca was all around me—strong body and wings and sharply contrasting face. His beauty stole my breath and sent throbbing heat between my legs.

"Do you believe in fate? Fated mates?" I whispered. *Say yes this time.*

"Is that your question?" His eyes were closed now.

"Yes."

"It's... That would be nice, but life isn't that easy. Perfect mates, fated mates, whatever you want to call them... The world's too complicated." He pinched my hip near the bruise.

"Maybe."

His strong arms tightened around my waist as his whole body surged closer to mine. With a low groan, he positioned me to straddle him. My layered green skirt hiked up around my hips. "For now, I can think of a way I'd be more comfortable."

My heart skittered. Wasn't the full moon still a week away? Usually, he didn't get this demanding until a couple days before. Honestly, I loved when he took control and lost control at once, but most of the time he didn't allow himself to. That bruise haunted him.

My thoughts melted away as his hot breath feathered over my mouth. His salty, cool scent filled my lungs the instant before his lips met mine. He kept his mouth resolutely closed until I opened for him, longing for the light scrape of his sharp teeth. But that was only ever when he lost control. The moon wasn't full yet.

One hand pressed my upper back and the other dominated my hip, pulling me up until I could feel his hard bulge against my pulsing core. Then he rocked us, grinding us together, rubbing my sensitive, wet clit.

His exhales became growls and grunts. Mine became whimpers. His bat-like wings contracted around us with arousal.

I rolled my hips faster in a circular motion we both went crazy for. Finally, he tore off the kiss and yanked my underwear to the side. Freeing his cock, he impaled me on it.

"Ah!" I cried, letting my head fall back as he thrust up in deeper and wilder strokes.

He licked a long line up my throat, then another, lapping up the sweat as we worked together, straining to get closer, to get friction on the sopping, swollen places.

I lost myself in him. There was his length inside me and his tongue on my neck and his strong, searching hands in my hair, on my ass, scratching my thighs, gripping my breasts...

My cries grew higher, higher. With a firm shove upward, he broke me. I exploded into blackened, piercing stars.

Luca was still feral, finishing, when I came to. Pulling out at the last moment, he shot cum on my lower belly.

Without him inside me, I could felt just how damn wet I was. My juices were getting all over Luca's tailored pants. But on full moon weeks, he never cared. On full moon weeks, like this one, he'd draw his finger across my pussy one more time and suck off the wet. Like he did now.

"Mmmm," he moaned. "You're the most delicious thing I've ever tasted, Juniper."

I flushed even hotter when he got all hoarse and wild like that. My name in his mouth sounded like sin.

"You cook every day," I teased.

Luca's lips curved, those expressive eyes dancing. "No spices taste like you, Jun."

Too bad he didn't believe in perfect mates, because I could have sworn he was mine.

I did believe in perfect mates. But Juniper couldn't know that.

What made her ask about mates at all? Did she think I was hers? My chest seized at the idea. Panic. Relief. I didn't know. Maybe both.

Did other vampires feel this same kind of panic when they *knew*? It couldn't be. Their mates could attend the full moon ritual. Vampires understood what it meant to surrender to the moon, to become one with the rest of our clan. Juniper, though...

No way in hell could I take Juniper to that. She was tough and smart and everything I ever wanted, but she was a faun. A faun in a sex-crazed horde of vampires was a very bad idea.

My chest ached. I rolled over toward Juniper to slow my racing thoughts. She slept peacefully in the darkness. If she opened her eyes, she wouldn't be able to see me. We'd tested that theory two years ago when we moved into this house. When I left my clan behind for this wonderful female.

I reached out, fingering her soft ear. Her anatomy fascinated me. Unlike vampires, her calves transitioned into a delicate hooves, and her ears poked up through her hair like small deer's. The rest resembled my smooth body, which yearned for hers right now.

I didn't need to see the moon to know how close it was to full. My heightened senses told me. The smell of Juniper, the sound of her heartbeat, the brush of her skin, the sight of her quick-talking little mouth, all drove me to distraction. I wanted to consume her. And that, of course, was part of the problem.

I reached into the bowl beside the bed and popped another salt bead. Never once had I broken my promise never to bite her, and I'd keep that promise as long as we were together. If I ever sensed my control slipping, I'd let her find happiness with someone else.

At the thought, I bared my fangs. Juniper was mine. No, that wasn't right. I was hers. My mind, my spirit, my entire godsdamned body knew it.

Even if she lived in another male's bed, I'd still be hers. I would watch her work in the Assembly, knowing she curled up with books about harpies or sirens at night to better understand and serve them. She kept my bedside bowl full of expensive salt beads, for Divine's sake.

If I could stay with her forever, I would. But Casimir would say that was my youth talking, the part that balked at reality. He was right.

I let my fingers trail to Juniper's shoulder. Her lips twitched into a half-smile. Pain shot through me at the look. Admitting the truth—that she was my perfect mate—would tether her to me, and I couldn't hold her back like that. I had responsibilities and urges she knew nothing about.

And I'd keep it that way.

I'd shown her as much as I could, but her question yesterday had me rattled, as if the hands of a moondial had started moving toward the end of a long, incredible night. It made me want to grab as much as I could before time ran out.

Many people even here in the dangerous Far Realm called vampires beasts. Right now, I'd agree we had beastliness in us. I remembered Juniper's bruise from last time moon energy coursed through me, and I still wanted to take her rough.

My stomach churned with anticipation as my urges surged up. Jun deserved love and kindness, but all my thoughts veered darker.

My length hardened at the mere memory of Juniper's sweat, the phantom sensation of licking her neck the other night.

"Juniper," I growled, crawling over her and caging her in. My leathery wings furled out above us.

She felt blindly at my forearm fisting the pillow near her head. "Luca?" A sleepy smile curled those delectable lips.

I dove for her and she squealed with pleasure.

That sound. My dick ached with the need to push inside her. Right now.

I scrabbled with her clothes and her hair. I was rough and I knew it, but I couldn't stop. Her sultry moans every time I touched her or grabbed her hair just made me more frenzied.

I panted, parting her legs. That soft inner thigh! Those knees pressed against my bare ass! The damp lips of her sex against the tip of my cock!

I was sensation and need. I needed Juniper. The inevitable end of us together only made my actions more urgent.

I found her hot, slick entrance and slid inside. She squeezed me, soaking me as I took our pleasure in deep thrusts.

Heavy and jagged, my breathing matched the relentless pace of fucking her. A kernel of a thought surfaced through the madness: Juniper likes when I pin her hands above her head. It helps her come.

With a snarl, I gripped both her wrists in one fist and slammed them against the headboard.

I came first. She wasn't far behind.

I collapsed next to her. We both smelled like sex and sweat. The delicious scent drew me closer to Juniper's trembling form. Her whole body glistened. I took my time licking the sweat from between her breasts, her collarbone, her stomach... Gods, she was a feast.

She sighed contently when I finished.

Blinking a few times to clear my mind—as much as it could clear—I observed her again. Her lips were parted as she gathered herself. She was so soft and small. Had I been too rough? I gnawed my lip with the point of my canine. With a gentle hand, I caressed the large bruise I'd left on her leg a month ago. I could still see it. Were there any more?

"Juniper..." But I had so little breath it came out a croak. "That was too much. I should have left this month. I'm sorry."

"No." She fished for my wrist. That whole experience had been blind for her. "I'm glad you stayed. You can go to the moon ritual whenever you want, but know that you can always stay with me too." Her whisper had that post-coital rasp that did nothing to calm my heart rate.

"You don't have to say that."

"I'm not just saying that. I like it when you get dirty." Her unfocused eyes looked a little crazy. I softened. Juniper was always thinking of others. That was one of the things I loved about her, but she didn't understand how deep vampire clan loyalty went. She'd gotten a glimpse of it when I chose to move and had days of brooding that wouldn't settle until I found a rhythm of returning to our ancestral land almost every month during the ritual.

I thumbed her bottom lip. "You don't know how dirty I can be." I'd meant it as a warning, but it sounded like an invitation. Damn full moon.

"I'd like to see," she said. "Would you take me to the next ritual?"

I almost choked on my own spit. The question sobered my sex-hazy brain as well as a plunge in an icy river. "Absolutely not. Vampires and fauns don't mix. You'd be in danger." She had no idea what she was asking. She'd never asked before. Why now?

Her brow furrowed. "They don't mix?"

My insides chilled. "*We* mix," I clarified, "but even demigods don't trespass on our lands during the full moon."

She pulled the blanket back up, snuggling it against her chin thoughtfully. She was cute, trying to be optimistic, as she usually was, but her ears tilted down. I'd hurt her. "Do you really think I'd be in danger if I went with you?"

I smoothed her blanket-covered shoulder. "It's not a safe place for you."

"But it's part of who you are. I want to know that part of you. It can be research. I would take precautions."

*That's the problem.* I didn't want her to know that side of me. It was feral and frightening. Other vampires understood what the moon did to us, but Juniper didn't need to.

If we weren't so secretive about full moon rituals, Juniper would already know everything from reading. Always studying different races with an eye to improve Nyx, to make it better for everyone in the Far Realm.

"You do know me," I insisted.

"But not this part."

Damn, she looked adorable all wrapped up like that. A precious being too good for the Far Realm. Too good for me.

She smacked her lips. "If you're afraid I'll see you with other vampires..."

"Juniper."

"I know you all get together and... But I've never been jealous. I knew you'd come back to me. It's just part of your culture."

"Juniper. You've been jealous." Returning after a ritual always left me spent. It was half exhilaration from reconnecting with my clan and half guilt for leaving Juniper behind to satisfy something selfish in me.

The blanket rose to her lips. "Only a little."

I folded my wings tighter against my back. "I'm sorry."

"Then take me with you next time."

"No."

She stiffened and angled up on her elbow. "Light a candle so I can see."

I did. She stared me down with those deep brown eyes. My

emotions roiled over each other—anger that she insisted on this, guilt that I couldn't give her what she wanted, fear that she'd see who I really was. Add to that a new hard on and I couldn't be reasonable.

"What's so terrible that I can't go?" she demanded.

"I don't want to talk about this."

"You can't even describe it for me."

"Leave it, Juniper."

Her eyes flew wide. "Leave it?" She sat up fully and crossed her arms. "I organized for human corpses to be transported here from the southern wharf just so the naga and other flesh-eating species could find a place in Nyx without harming other citizens. You really think your culture is so awful that I won't be able to handle it?"

I ran a hand over my face. "That's different. You're not in bed with a naga." My body was starting to zing with the need for movement—to fight, to fuck.

I really should have left this month. The so-called "demon room" at the inn wasn't good enough. I had to be gone for more than just one night.

"No," she agreed. "I'm in bed with you, and I don't understand why you're hiding things from me."

"You know the full moon is in a couple days," I growled in warning.

She pulled her shoulders back. "I know."

"Then don't push this." I swallowed, trying to recenter. I loved Juniper. So why was I acting like such an asshole? I didn't want to talk to her this way, but she kept prodding at the part of me that would scare her off. I couldn't show her, or I'd lose her more quickly. "Please, Juniper, don't push this."

She grimaced, her chest swelling more quickly with hurt. I could make it swell and shudder more. I could make those nipples harden and her full hips contract around me...

She uncrossed her arms. I ran a hand over the front of her body, tracing the lines of her breasts and belly. She released a deep breath and lightly placed a fist against my chest.

"I know I frustrate you," I said, low and deep, lowering my hand and kneading her sex.

She pounded her fist against me. "Yes."

"Do that again."

She hit harder.

I groaned.

The next time she tried, I caught her wrist and we were wrestling, saying everything without words. What I was and who I loved didn't match, and it was fucking frustrating. She grabbed my hair and my neck, twisting in my grasp but staying under me.

The moon took me again. We were fighting but magnetic. We couldn't let go, always touching, clutching at each other as if we'd be pulled apart. I wrung pleasure from her by force. She was gasping, scratching my back near my wings, straining to keep herself together but exploding in shuddering orgasms. I knew what she liked and I took and took. More and more. Until we were deliciously sweat-soaked and the night ran out.

"You seem distracted, Juniper."

I blinked and looked down at Noula. Her huge black eyes had struck me as bug-like when I first met her as part of my city development team, but now I saw the intelligent compassion in them. She fluttered her thin wings. They matched her skeletally thin body, a head shorter than me.

"Maybe I am," I admitted. I'd been staring at the same piece of paper for who knew how long. I focused on it again. Underground species were compromising the integrity of buildings, it alleged. I sighed.

"Normally, you fly through your work faster than anyone here," Noula said. She touched me with one pointed finger.

"It's nothing."

Noula pursed her little mouth, making her eyes look even bigger. I tried to ignore her, but she wasn't making that easy.

"Fine," I said, setting down the paper on a nearby desk. The structural integrity of buildings in the best city of the most diverse and dangerous realm in the known world was more important than troubles in my love life, but I gave in. "I had an argument with Luca a couple days ago."

"The vampire."

It wasn't a question, just a clarification, but my skin prickled as if she'd criticized me. Maybe I was just used to having to explain myself. A faun with a vampire? It did sound pretty ludicrous.

"Yes," I confirmed. "You share big life experiences with your partners, right?"

"I suppose."

As far as I knew, Noula didn't have one steady partner, so maybe it was different for her.

"Have you ever loved someone?" I asked. "You know, been with them a long time because you want to learn more about them, and hear what they think, and spend your nights sitting together even if you aren't talking? Something that goes beyond sex, but that part's good too? Have you ever thought, 'My chest hurts with the size of the love inside'?" I blinked. My bottom lids were wet.

"Juniper..." Noula crooned, leading me to a chair. It was too tall for me, made for the deathless gods and demi-gods, so I had to give a little jump to get into the red embroidered seat. Noula fluttered up to the armrest so she could look me in the eye. "You're in love with Luca."

I swallowed and nodded.

"Doesn't he love you back?" The way she phrased the question left me uneasy. Sprites, with their expert illusions, had the unfair reputation as liars and manipulators. I didn't think Noula meant to manipulate me with the question, but my skin did that prickly thing again. I shouldn't have been uneasy. Of course Luca loved me. He'd left his clan to live with me in the north.

"I think so," I answered.

"Hm," Noula squeaked. "What was your argument about? Can I send him spiders? Tentacles?"

"No, he didn't do anything wrong." I sighed. "He won't let me go to the full moon ritual."

Noula's tiny mouth fell open.

"I know. I know. But his whole family goes every month. All the vampires do. And I'm just trying to get to know him."

"The full moon ritual? Juniper, you've heard what happens there."

Warmth rushed to my cheeks. "Luca goes most months. I don't mind."

"You wouldn't mind getting railed by an entire vampire clan, not just your boyfriend?" Noula gave her wings a shake. "I probably wouldn't mind either, if I could survive it." She turned her serious gaze on me. "But that's the problem, Juniper. I see why he said no."

My ears twitched. "If I'm willing to try, he should let me." I frowned at the memory of his command. Luca was usually so understanding. Lately, though, his favorite word was no.

"You know about the ritual," Noula said. "That should be enough."

I gestured at the bookshelves built into the wall behind us. "No one knows the full truth except the vampires who go. There are secrets."

"Everyone has secrets," she interrupted.

"This just seems like a big one. Maybe that's why I'm upset.

For a long time, I didn't care. It was his heritage, not mine. But now..." I took a deep breath. "I think he's my perfect mate. If this is forever, then I need to know."

"Perfect mate." She rolled her huge eyes. "Spoken like a vampire. Are you going to drink blood now?"

I pushed her off the armrest. "Noula! You know better than to say that."

She fluttered to regain her balance. "You're right. But you are sounding like a vampire."

A tiny part of me, deep inside, glowed. I wanted to be a faun and a vampire, just like I wanted Luca to be a vampire and a faun. I wanted us to understand each other deep down in our bones.

I tried one of his salt beads once. It was tasty, but he sucked them more often than I'd want to, so I left the rest for him.

"He's never threatened to do that," I said. "He's always protected me, even on the day we first met in Aridian. I was visiting family and doing research on lycans."

"Let me guess. You were alone."

I chewed my lip. "I had just started this job and you know how I get. I want to know everything. I wanted to see what kind of accommodation they might benefit from. I wasn't going to stay, just see where they lived and observe from a distance."

Judging from her face, Noula already knew where this story was going.

"This"—I exhaled—"beautiful male walked through the woods. He startled me. I didn't expect anyone else to be there. We ended up talking." I dropped my eyes. "Well, he warned me to get out of there before the lycans started prowling around. And he was so easy to talk to. I basically told him everything about my job and how proud I was to get the position."

"And that you want to run the Assembly someday," Noula supplied.

"Yes. I asked him all about his family. I think he was surprised I wasn't afraid of him. But he was so nice, and we... Well, we've been together since that day. It's like I knew the minute I saw him."

"After he popped out of the woods."

"Yes. He showed me things I never knew about the Aridian Forest, even though I'd grown up near there. Habitats and the way species interact..."

When I looked up, Noula was staring at me.

"I don't know why this is where he draws the line." I kicked my hooves. "He said he didn't believe in perfect mates," I added in a mutter.

Noula inhaled sharply. "He doesn't believe in perfect mates? Juniper... I'm sorry."

I didn't like that *I'm sorry*. It sounded too much like *He's going to end things*. Would he really do that? After all we'd been through?

When I was anxious about King Hades' upcoming visit to oversee how the Assembly was managing Nyx, Luca bought me two gifts—a plant for the house and ginger candies to settle my stomach.

Luca held my shuddering body as I cried over the death of my aunt.

Luca protected me from a Harpy who came screeching out

of the trees on a research trip. Wings and blood went everywhere. I was a peace-loving vegetarian, but seeing Luca's blood-streaked face after he defended me made me want to rip off his clothes right there. It happened a year ago, but I still thought about that moment all the time. Often when Luca was gone at the ritual and I had the bed to myself.

"Everyone's different," I said, echoing a common refrain. But Noula was right. Maybe Luca did believe in perfect mates. He just had stopped believing in me.

# LUCA

I stirred the walnut and mushroom stew, watching tendrils of steam waft around the wooden spoon. Thyme leaves and red wine finished off this portion for Juniper. Hopefully she'd like it. In another pan, I seared pieces of mutton. Those were for my bowl.

Even our meals couldn't fully blend.

Juniper had already left for work by the time I returned home earlier today, exhausted by my night away. Emergency lodging for one night was sometimes better than a full trip back to my clan in Sosnekrev—even if I did have to stay in a "demon room."

Ignorant people laughed at locked-door guesthouses, like the one where I worked. But we all lived in the Far Realm, for gods' sake. They should have known better than to underestimate the need for more secure lodgings. Vampires weren't the only ones who became unpredictable without an outlet.

Juniper could probably list them all, and what each species needed. The most incredible thing was how she was curious without judgment. My upbringing taught a hierarchy it was hard to shake, and so did hers, yet here she was. She knew where I went for the full moon and never scolded me for being myself. The more I talked about vampires, the more her brown eyes widened in fascination. At facts that made other people squirm, Juniper just took notes and asked questions.

I bit my lower lip lightly with my pointed canine. The food was almost done.

Exhaling, I lifted both pans off the heat. With hinges creaking, the iron stove door opened to let air in so the wood would burn more slowly.

At the same moment, our front door opened too. A quiet series of rattles unique to Juniper. The sound was as familiar as a voice.

I pushed the walnut and mushroom stew around to its most appetizing configuration. Smoothing back my hair, I met her coming into the kitchen.

My senses flared at her entrance. She wore a trim brown bodice beneath a jacket and a simple green skirt.

"Mmmm," she crooned. "What's this?" She took a big sniff of the scented air. The grin that usually accompanied exclamations like that didn't reach her eyes.

I eased her jacket off and caressed her smooth shoulder. "Your favorite, Jun."

I could tell she was happy with the meal, but something else bothered her.

*Please, not the full moon ritual.* The full moon was over, so we should get a few peaceful weeks, at least.

I hated thinking of us as week to week. But what else could

I do? I'd stay with Juniper as long as I could—make the most of it—until I couldn't anymore.

Was two years that limit?

My insides churned at the idea. No, not the idea, the *knowledge*. I'd have to give up my perfect mate. Rip out part of myself and find a way to live broken.

I served food for us both and fetched a bottle of wine. Together, we sat at the wooden table her father had carved for her. Last year, I'd come home to find the backrest sanded down on the sides so I didn't have splay my wings against it.

Juniper tucked into her meal immediately. Her bronze hair curled around her ear as she dipped her head. "Thank you. This is great. It's been a long day."

"Has it?" I took a bite of meat. I'd seasoned it, but it didn't taste like anything.

"Maybe I was tired. I didn't sleep much last night."

"Neither did I."

Awkward silence blanketed the table. This wasn't right. This wasn't *us*.

I set down my cutlery. "I was thinking about you. You understand why I didn't invite you to the full moon ritual, don't you?"

She hummed, not looking up from her meal. From the rate she was eating, she either loved the stew or was feeling even more uncomfortable than I was.

"I could tell you more about it, if you want. Then it might be clearer."

That got her attention.

Encouraged, I went on. "It's not right to hang our peace on

this one question—whether you can go do something dangerous."

Her expression pinched with irritation. "Maybe I can decide if it's dangerous for me once you tell me more," she said tightly.

I didn't like this dance. She was right. I couldn't dictate her life. But I did know vampires, and full moons, and what she might think of me if she saw it all in front of her. I couldn't win either way.

"I... That's true," I conceded.

She raised her eyebrows.

"You can't write this down for the Assembly."

"How long have I been dating a vampire?"

I smirked. "Long enough. There are rules for the ritual."

Her bright eyes couldn't contain her excitement. Gods, I loved her. She deserved to know I wasn't good enough for her. Vampires had prestige, but not her level of care and goodness.

I raised a finger. "One from every immediate family, for obvious reasons. We rotate."

She nodded, fisting her hands as if physically stopping herself from recording my exact words for research.

I shuffled through all those nights, the snap of autumn and the glow of summer heat. Snowy moons were my favorite. "There's a place in the heart of our territory. We don't allow anyone else to set foot in it. It's sacred. A clearing, where we can see the sky."

I took another bite. What details would satisfy her and also help her understand my position without giving away everything?

"There are blood cisterns along one edge." I treated the

round table like the clearing and planted three fingers to demonstrate.

She swallowed her next bite more thickly. "Cisterns?" she repeated, grimacing. "Wouldn't that...?"

"More like buckets, really. We only fill them up once a month."

"Okay. What do you use them for?"

I hadn't gotten her to shy away with one of the more grotesque features of the ritual. I should have known. "Our bites have become too dangerous, even painful for ourselves sometimes, so we needed a different way." I paused.

"Like the salt beads."

"Exactly."

"So you... drink it?" Small lines around her mouth were the only sign of how disgusted she was.

"No," I said, relieved for some reason. "We have different ages of maturity. You know that. And some decide to wait for a long time before joining the ritual. Anyway, once vampires are fully grown, they must attend a year of rituals as an acolyte. They're in charge of the blood. The... painting." Satisfied I'd chosen the right word, I repeated it.

"I didn't picture painting there," she mused.

I rushed on before she could ask any more questions. "There are high platforms as well. Mostly for sacrifices."

"Sacrifices?" she snapped.

"We don't kill them. We don't kill anyone. Well, animals for the blood." I veered away from the sacrifices. Most vampires joining for the first time had to act as sacrifice first before they could join the rest below. "At full dark, we all converge for the ritual. And that's it. We go all night, or until we're exhausted." I put another bite between my lips and glanced up at Juniper, who appeared to be digesting all the information I'd told her. It was more than I'd ever divulged before.

"Is the ritual only sex?"

I coughed delicately at her question. How could I answer? It felt like so much more than that, closeness to my clan and my culture, to the moon and the mad parts inside me that my community embraced. She made it sound wrong.

"Basically."

"But you don't want me there?"

Her question stabbed like a fang. The only person I wanted in my bed was her. The person I wanted most in my life was her. If she didn't agree to let me return to my clan, knowing the ritual was essentially an orgy, I would have listened. No more trips to Sosnakrev. I would have stayed in one of those godsdamned "demon rooms" every time.

"Do you not want me to go next month?" I asked.

"Luca..." She scooched her chair around the table to be closer to mine. "Go. I won't hold you back." There was a strange mix of expressions on her face. It made me uncomfortable.

I hated this week. Why was Juniper suddenly slipping from my grasp? Compulsively, I put my hand over hers, as if that could stop that from happening.

"I love you, Luca."

My throat balled into a fierce pain. She watched me with eager eyes. Inside, it was easy: *I love you too.*

At that moment, I wished I could be anything other than a vampire. Fuck these traditions and the weight we put on those words. They were words for a mate. They bubbled inside me, trying to force their way out.

In a flash of clarity, I saw our likely future. Months would mark another measure of distance between us whether I stayed or left. I'd run out of information to give her, and she'd get tired of waiting for nothing. Our families weren't especially happy with our choice to be with each other. That friction would wear us away as surely as rough stone wore away skin.

Our relationship was dying.

My breathing grew shallow.

...What if I did invite Juniper to the next full moon ritual? What was the worst that could happen?

I popped a salt bead into my mouth with the next tasteless bite of meat, even though I knew I'd already over-salted it.

Juniper could be ridiculed, bitten, hurt. She could see me at my most primal and stop loving me. A thousand things could go wrong.

But which was worse? The slow, painful death of a relationship with the person I desperately loved, or exploding it all at once—showing her the truth?

At the ritual, I could still try to protect her from physical harm. I was never so far gone I could forget something that crucial.

"You won't love me soon," I murmured. If only I could shut out the whole world to keep Juniper. But she respected me too much to let me do that.

Her glossy eyes locked on mine. She just shook her head, brown curls bouncing around her forehead. How could she be so sure?

I gave her a kiss.

"Next month," I began slowly, "let's go together."

She spoke so close it almost felt like another kiss. "Are you sure?"

I wasn't sure. But a twisted part of me reveled in the idea, now that I had it, of showing Juniper that night. Would it turn her on? Would she get any ideas to make life better for vampires in Nyx? Would my family accept her after all?

At the thought of my family, concerns welled up again.

"We'll be careful," I answered. It was the best I could do. I was a mess, half-hard at the thought of Juniper joining us, but unable to confess how deeply I loved her, and how devastated I'd be once she was gone.

❧ 5 ❧

# JUNIPER

I expected blood. I expected some resistance to my being in vampire territory.

I did not expect a faun delegation to arrive on my last day of work before the trip. Today was supposed to be routine. Basic tasks, getting everything ready for my absence which would take a few days...

These fauns hadn't made an appointment. I wasn't supposed to have any consultations, but I had to keep my demeanor pleasant and helpful. I shouldn't have been nervous, but the sudden appearance of four fauns felt like a sign. A sign of what, I didn't know, but I felt defensive, for some reason.

Noula eyed me, wings fluttering, as I ushered them into the Forest Room. I gave her a blank, happy stare back.

"I'm so glad they have a faun working here at the Assembly," said the fatherly-looking leader with horns and round glasses. "I thought it would be all demi-gods with their shapes and sizes."

He made "shapes and sizes" sound like a bad thing. My hackles rose.

"Do you want to take a seat?" I asked, gesturing to the stump-like stools around a wooden table. *Don't judge them too quickly. Be what you want to see.* "What brings you in today?"

Noula settled weightlessly at my side as I sat.

"But this is a high position," continued the fatherly faun, gazing around the large room where dark bookshelves lined the walls and the ceiling had been painted to look like tall fir trees reaching to a star-strewn night sky. "That's good. That's very good."

"Yes, I earned it by being a good accessibility researcher," I answered tightly. "I'm happy to represent fauns this way."

"Lord Hades is open-minded. It's others who sometimes prevent us from getting ahead." He didn't look at Noula, but I could tell she felt like an outsider in this conversation.

I sucked in a slow breath. "That's true. Can I help you with something? There must be a reason why you're here."

The other three fauns deferred to the leader. They looked meek, timid even. I acted a little like them growing up, before I untangled my cultural expectations and took the good threads with me: loyalty, optimism, work ethic. Strangely, I didn't spend a lot of time with other fauns now.

Luca sat right behind my ribcage like a secret. He wasn't. We weren't. But I recognized the tone of someone who would grimace with distaste if I revealed the truth.

"I'll get straight to the point," the fatherly one said. "Our neighborhood has been experiencing difficulties. I tell everyone to stay indoors at night. Don't go out alone."

The faun over his shoulder nodded.

There were lots of rough neighborhoods in Nyx. It was a beautiful city that spoke to my soul, but it had its share of problems. Growing pains, I told myself, for the wonderful place it would one day become. A place where even outcast demi-gods could be welcome, as long as they followed some basic rules of respecting one another.

I waited for the faun to go on.

"There's a mother with five children who lives across the street whose husband was killed. I don't know how she gets what she needs. Well, I do know. It's the four of us who bring her food and the things she asks for. She pays us back. We tell her she doesn't need to pay the full amount—"

"Is there," I interrupted as politely as possible, "is there a reason you didn't go to the protection department?" Clearly, a threat was what he was leading up to, some reason why fauns weren't safe in his area.

"No no no. We couldn't go there. You understand us better. We're not helpless. We just need help."

I did understand that. Pursing my lips, I nodded for him to go on.

"It's Aber, the demi-goddess." His words lifted at the end like a question. Had I heard of her?

I nodded again. Aber didn't usually cause trouble, at least when she was left alone. She had an area of deep tide pools and caves where she lived with her servant-worshippers. Her dwelling wasn't officially in Nyx, but down the eastern coast.

"The Aber-suna has spread out of control. They think it's a game to snatch sacrifices for her," he huffed.

Suna were cults to deathless beings who didn't officially

rule. Hades, god of the dead, was King of the Far Realm. For most, that was enough, especially since the truce on Eriset meant there were fewer dead humans sent to the docks, freeing Hades to rule more hands-on throughout the rest of the Realm. His powers terrified everyone, but most of us knew he ruled fairly. Hades even spoke Hingat. But suna weren't unheard of. Sometimes people wanted to pray to a god of health, for instance. Vampires had beliefs about the moon as the source of elemental power or beingness or something like that. Since Luca never discussed it, the explanation slipped my mind. I had to ask on our way to the clan.

"No one should be snatching sacrifices," I declared. "I'll report it to the protection department immediately."

One of the meek fauns behind the speaker piped up. "They have wild parties," she said. "They make mazes and drink and then laugh when we walk by."

My heart twisted. They were prey in their own neighborhood. "Where do you live?"

Noula helped me take down their information.

The fauns all nodded and thanked me multiple times even though I hadn't done anything yet. Working with the protection department wasn't something new to me. We'd had meetings before. Usually, I suggested something non-violent on one end of the table, and the other person argued for something more efficient. I respected the protection department, but we didn't always see eye to eye.

"Aber," the fatherly one scoffed as he got to his feet. "Just because she's tall and beautiful... She sucks blood like a vampire, you know. Cleans them dry. She's a maneater."

My chest seized. "Vampires don't do that anymore, you

know." I hadn't mean to say it. It was irrelevant to this meeting, but now that the words had escaped my mouth, I straightened, ready to defend them.

"They do," said one of the others. "I had a cousin who *saw* one do it."

"Think about it." The leader peered at me through his glasses. "We're too quick to trust vampires these days. You need to keep an eye on them. Happens every year." He said it as if he were the teacher and I were the student.

"It's happened four times in the last ten years, and two of those were the same offender," I said, fighting to keep my voice even. "I'd appreciate it if you didn't make sweeping judgments here."

Noula put her little hand on my upper arm. I ignored her warning.

"I don't know where you're getting your information, but I'm telling you, they go rogue more often than that. Vampires see fauns as prey. Don't let their faces fool you."

"Juniper..." Noula whispered.

My face felt hot and my ears went back. "I'm getting my information from years of research, and from my boyfriend, who is a vampire, and who has always been kind to me. I'll pass along your complaint. Next time, if the suna bothers you, talk to the protection department. Have a good day."

Without looking back, I stalked out of the room to my office.

This edginess had something to do with the full moon ritual approaching. I knew it. I was already on edge with excitement and apprehension about the trip. Luca's standoffishness the past month crawled around under my skin, adding an extra layer of nerves. There were moments when it felt like he was going to break things off, or say he didn't love me. They were quick, half-seconds, but my blood would go ice-cold.

And now this well-meaning but ignorant faun telling me about how vampires were bad. It plucked a string I'd heard too many times. I would choose Luca a thousand times more, but I was tired of standing up for him. For us. I wanted Luca to show he was fighting for me too.

After all, getting snippy with people I was here to help wouldn't win me any favors with the Assembly. I wanted changes *now*, as fast as I could learn and implement, but governing, even in a great city like Nyx, didn't go that fast.

People like that faun picking at scabs that were trying to heal only made me more impatient. If only people could see that all beings mattered, that we had so many important things in common, and we just needed some individual consideration, everything would be better.

Noula called me idealistic. That was true. Optimistic, sure. Both qualities that would make me a good leader of the Assembly, not a bad one.

I picked at my lip. Did I even have a chance to make that dream come true?

To be leader of the Assembly one day.

To hear Luca say I was his perfect mate.

My sparkling optimism faded. With a deep breath, I shut my eyes tight. Noula wasn't in here, so she wouldn't see me talking to myself.

"You can do it, Juniper. You can be the first faun leading the Assembly." I exhaled. "You'll go to the ritual with Luca and find out if he's truly in love with you." Wetness squeezed between my closed eyelids. "I know he cares, but that's not enough. Either he loves me enough to fight for me, or..." I hesitated, knotting my fingers together and clasping so hard my hands started to shake. "Or I move on. Perfect mates aren't one-sided." I sniffed. "Perfect mates are not one-sided."

# JUNIPER

Luca stopped short in the doorway.

I stuffed books into my satchel as quickly as I could, but he caught me.

"This isn't going to be like the river hike, is it?" he asked.

"This trip is nothing like that one. We won't be doing as much walking."

"I carried your books the entire way."

"Not the first part! And I could have carried them, but they were slowing us down, so you were kind and took them."

He groaned, but he was smiling. His eyes couldn't hide anything.

So it was hard to shake the feeling I'd seen something dark in those kind eyes a few weeks ago when he invited me. On the one hand, he was letting me in at last. The ritual sounded primal and terrifying, but exciting. On the other hand, he'd invited me grudgingly. I wanted him to feel free to do as he liked, just as he wanted for me, I thought. I tried not to worry about that look, the one that sank his eyes to grief.

The memory soured the pit of my stomach, so I picked up my largest volume—the one Luca had bought me our first year together, about the known world's creatures. It was so thick I had trouble balancing the spine in my hand. "Do you think I'll need this one?" I teased.

"I don't think you'll need any of them. You can't reveal new information you find, remember? This is just for us."

*Just for us.* I liked the sound of that. And I liked the look of him in the doorway, all broody-looking with those unfurled bat wings. He held a cup of salty tea.

I set down the book. I hadn't really planned to bring that tome, but I'd be damned if I couldn't bring notebooks. Vampires were letting me into the heart of their society. It was a rare privilege. I'd note all the ways they accommodated their wings in shared spaces, the methods of slaking their bloodlust without hurting anyone, even the way the interacted with each other. In Nyx and the rest of the Far Realm, vampires appeared in ones and twos, not in whole clans. My heart charged with anticipation.

"I wrote to the leader of my clan to let them know you're coming," he said. "I reminded them to be nice."

I harumphed and fastened the clasp on my packed satchel. "Thank you, but they don't need to be nice."

"Well..." His intense gaze raked from my bronze curls to my hooves. Everything in between looked vampire-like, not like some little forest animal, which was still how some people treated fauns. One look at my ears or one word I said in my slight Hingat accent and they'd purse their mouths, all thought gone of taking me seriously. *Why can't we all move past our differ-*

*ences?* I thought for the millionth time, but Luca's eyes were distracting. And lingering...

"We can have fun with this," I said cheerily, trying to rub off my stress sweat without Luca noticing. It was useless. He smelled sweat on me before I even noticed it. In bed, it was sexy. Eating at his restaurant, it was a little embarrassing.

He chuckled. "Fun?"

"It's... like a party."

He grinned, gaze dropping, and set down his tea.

This month's full moon was only a couple days away. It had gotten colder and brighter every night. Sweet handholding had turned into Luca pinning me against every surface in the house. Except for Luca's shame about the whole thing (which was totally undeserved), and the fact he had to leave for a while around the full moon itself, I secretly loved his transformation.

I had to admit I had butterflies thinking about staying with him on the actual day of the ritual, though. He did get more combative when the moon was full. And I'd be not only with him, but an entire vampire clan. During the ritual.

"Something wrong?" he asked, approaching and tipping my head up not by my chin, but by my throat. Still, his touch was gentle. He caressed my neck with his thumb.

When I didn't answer, he said, "I hope you do have fun." Then his expression showed a thousand things I couldn't quite interpret—amusement, doubt, encouragement, admiration. His expressiveness never failed to make me weak for him. Watching him, especially when he let his guard down, was endlessly fascinating.

"We're doing it now," I said with a sort of chirpy, optimistic seriousness. "We're going. You've told the vampires we'll be there."

"Juniper." His tone became so serious that I straightened. He opened his mouth, closed it. A secret burned in his eyes and then faded like a flame. "Don't be nervous. You insisted on seeing this side of me, remember?"

I released a breath. "Yes. I like your different sides."

"Mmm, I like your different sides."

Taking my cue, I sashayed in a circle, giving him a good view of my thick hips. He drank in the sight. Growling again, he snatched me and held me against him. I yelped but didn't try to escape. I couldn't if I wanted to. And I didn't. I wanted his strong arms pressing me against his body while he whispered filthy things in a voice of silk against my ear.

Even if his chest felt a little too stiff and his words sounded a little too frenzied. In two years, I'd learned a lot about Luca. And something was off with him.

"You know what I want?" he hissed. "I want you to ride my cock, bounce that ass in front of me. You want vampire dick that leaves you bruised, don't you?"

I forgot everything else I was thinking. I nodded, and he flew into action. I moved my satchel out of the way just in time for him to fling me on the bed.

A quarter hour later, my butt cheeks stung with Luca's handprints. He took me rough, and I took him rough.

He met my eyes. His hunger hadn't subsided. For a few days a month, Luca was insatiable. I kissed him, holding in a groan when his fingers gripped my bare hips. A new, deep bruise ached there. At least I could cover this one up easily. He didn't say it, but I knew Luca feared not only hurting me in moments like this, but hurting me in a way that people could see. Neither of us wanted to support the false belief that I was weak and he couldn't control his violence.

When I could think like a rational person again, nerves rose like bubbles. How would Luca act with the full moon hanging above us? Could I take it? Could I take an entire *clan*?

A seed of doubt sprouted in my chest.

*You can do it, Juniper. You are the future leader of the Assembly, the researcher, the one who loves Luca the vampire, even on full moons.*

I liked long walks, and it was a good thing, because we had to trek most of the way through the Far Realm wilderness to Sosnakrev. The weather was turning cold, which meant fewer dangers. Whether or not I liked to admit it, vampires—including my family—comprised the main ones. Compared to them, the odd harpy or naga didn't sound frightening.

For this walk, I'd donned a long jacket and boots, as well as a knife for protection. Really, I brought the blade for Juniper's benefit, to show I'd protect her. I didn't need it to fend off most predators. Fangs would do.

With every step, my heritage tugged at me. Every shade of blood and moonlight and tradition. It was odd to feel such closeness to my vampire roots and such apprehension and annoyance at the same time. Even my thoughts started to mirror a vampire's formal speech patterns. In Nyx, I'd taken to speaking more informally. It wasn't until I'd gone home for the full moon ritual a few months after moving in with Juniper that someone pointed out how I'd changed. I sounded younger, they said, and more naïve.

I took that last statement as a compliment, because they meant more open-minded. Maybe even idealistic. I got all that from Juniper.

As we strode over pine needle covered paths, Juniper wasn't as talkative as usual, though her gaze still observed everything with bright curiosity. She wore a sleek paneled skirt and a nicer shirt than she usually wore on hikes. Across her shoulder was her pack with extra clothes and, inevitably, her notebook.

Juniper loved adventure if there was learning involved. She'd always been dorky and brave and wonderful like that.

And I was bringing her to the most feral day for vampires. Why had I said yes?

*Because you want her to know.*

I set my teeth in my mouth and cheated another look at her. She took two steps for every one of mine. Those little faun hooves... When I scanned back up to her face, her eyes looked too far ahead. I knew that look.

"Getting nervous?" I asked. Both the fancy shirt and thoughtful gaze gave her away.

She adjusted the strap of her bag over her shoulder. "I'm not nervous."

"You're a little bit nervous. Or you should be."

She cocked an eyebrow at me. "How much farther? I've never been all the way into your woods."

I scanned the area around us, itching to palm the handle of my knife. Defending us would feel useful, at least.

An unwanted, defensive thought bubbled up. *I've never*

*been to Sprig to meet your family either.* My insides roiled. Juniper had never met anyone in my family. It was safer that way.

I met a sister of Juniper's once. It went... okay.

For the thousandth time, I doubted my decision to let her come. At the new moon, this trip would have made more sense. Less moon energy to dig into the wildest parts of our souls. We were more sedate then—the icy-calm vampires people pictured when they thought of us.

"About two hours at this pace, I think," I answered.

Jun was quiet. It wasn't like her. It put my already edgy thoughts into a swirl of chaotic uncertainty. It didn't help that the moon was waxing by the second.

"Talk me through it," she said softly.

"Hm?"

"Talk me through my part. Where will I be?"

I took in her earnest brown eyes. Something besides this trip bothered her. Was it the same uneasiness that haunted me?

"You will be with me," I began, lowering my voice.

Would she, though? They wouldn't make her follow vampire rules despite being a faun, would they? The idea hit me like a punch. Vampires went from tending to the blood, to one month of moon sacrifice, to full participation. I didn't like any option where she wasn't by my side. The younger ones only helped and observed. The sacrifices were dedicated to the moon and her power. No one could consummate with them unless...

I cleared my throat. "I'll be with you for everything except the entrance. We come in on different sides."

Her hand floated to her bag as if she wanted to write that down, but she lowered it again. "Why?"

"Females take something before going in."

A bit of the strain around her mouth relaxed.

"Families are important to vampires," I went on. "You mentioned the other day about perfect mates. Most of us believe in them. Many extend that importance to families as well. So, if someone got pregnant at the ritual, no one would know who the... who the father was. As far as I know, all of you will take precautions before it starts."

"I see." She had that interview look now, penetrating and curious. The kind of look that meant nothing else mattered besides this conversation.

When I first met her in the woods that day, she caught my eye, but it was this look that placed me permanently under her spell. I'd been hers ever since. Elders talked about what it felt like to meet their perfect mate and *know* their body, soul, and mind would always be theirs. I wasn't sure I believed them. They described something so intense, almost fairytale-like. But five minutes after meeting Juniper, I knew they were right. In my balls, in my bones, in my deepest held beliefs, I was hers.

I would always be hers, even after she was someone else's. The thought brought rage roaring up through my chest, but a thousand reasons made that outcome inevitable.

"And then what?" she prompted.

I slowed my breathing, a technique my uncle had taught me. He worked in Lord Hades' palace now, so he knew how to control himself well enough. "Drums. Drums signal the beginning."

"And then...?"

Images of bodies and blood, of moonlight and snow and flesh and abandon, filled my mind. "And then, you lose yourself to the moon." I slid my gaze away.

"Now, what does that mean?" Her prim tone marked a huge shift from the salacious direction my thoughts were going.

I drew a salt bead from my pocket and sucked. "You've studied vampires and the moon. She is life, energy at its most elemental."

"The deep parts of yourself? Like when you stop thinking?"

"Something like that. It's almost like soul. Wildness. Your individual life and the lives of others. What makes alive things alive." This was hard to explain. Hopefully Juniper understood.

"So, when you abandon yourself to the moon," she mused, "are you acting only on instinct?"

I snapped. "Yes!" Smiling, I gave her a salty kiss. "That's exactly it. Primal instinct."

"Does that please the moon?"

Her question threw me. "What? No. The moon is central to life. We're just aligned to her. She's not like a goddess. Like"—I cast around for an example—"like Queen Persephone who could choose to grow a tree over there." I pointed at the damp earth off the path. It was starting to drizzle. "The moon is... different, older."

Juniper nodded. For a few more steps, we said nothing.

"Luca," she said, slipping her hand in mine.

I readjusted my wings. Even after more than two years together, her touch set my limbs on fire.

"Will it bother you if I do what everyone else is doing? If other people touch me?"

I swallowed the last of the bead. I'd asked myself the question and could never quite force my heart into the right answer. "I hope not," I answered honestly. "It shouldn't."

"Well, I know I'll hate seeing you with other vampires."

I laughed in shock, even as my heart dropped. "What? You let me go every month."

"But I don't have to watch. I don't mind that you do it, but if I'm being..."

"Primal?"

"...with another vampire while you're doing someone else over there, I think I'll go crazy. I'll be jealous."

"What if your vampire's better at it than I am?" I teased. This whole conversation felt like a hallucination.

"Impossible." Her quick word sent pleasurable heat to my chest. "What if your vampire satisfies you more?"

"Impossible. It hasn't happened before. It won't happen now." Something about her little, earnest curves held me captive.

"You'll stay with me?"

I nodded, drawing her close. My skin warmed with her touch. Her bronze curls sparkled in the wet, but hadn't lost their shape. "I'll stay with you." The scent of her sweat rose through the chill and made me dizzy with lust.

"I might still be jealous, but I'll try to be good," she said, her tone a mix of flirtation and nervous determination.

"I hope not," I growled, easing our packs off our shoulders and setting them under a tree. My tenuous grip on self-control slipped, but only the faintest voice inside me cared.

My black wings flared and curled forward as I pushed Juniper against the nearest big trunk. Her cheeks flushed as she gazed up at me, inviting. Gods, she knew how to turn me on just by... being. She fit in my soul and in my arms. I fit between her legs.

"Just be you," I said, my breath blowing in her face. "Don't try to be good."

My dick pulsed as I drew it out and raised her skirt. This time, it was just the two of us. I didn't want any preamble. I wanted to let my nerves and energy loose while we were still alone. Before I had to face my family and protect Juniper from harm.

She was warm and wet and ready for me.

"Are you going to be bad for me, Jun?" I rumbled, plunging deep inside.

She grimaced and nodded.

I pushed in deeper, grinding in a circle. "How bad?"

She puffed out a panted breath against my neck.

"How bad?" My thrusts grew harder, pressing her hips against the tree.

Her mouth opened, tongue out. Whatever I'd do to her, she'd take.

*Danger!* said that small part of me. But it was drowned out by the piercing ache in my cock and the smell of Juniper's sweat.

I spit in her mouth. She swallowed. A half-snarl, half-laugh ripped from my throat. I ground against her more relentlessly. "That's it. Take what I give you."

Already, her hot, sopping pussy was about to make me come. But I wanted to hear her scream first. If I just sank my teeth into her neck, I could—

No. Couldn't break her.

But her blood would taste so good.

I channeled my frustration, my maddening arousal into my thrusts. I rotated her a little so my searching fingers could find her clit. She was swollen. When I rubbed, her belly against mine contracted with uneven breaths.

I grinned, savage, and doubled down on the rhythm with drenched fingers. Soon, she ground against me too. We rocked together, chasing release.

"Show me, Jun," I ground out. "Come on my cock."

Her face twitched.

"Yes, come on my fingers."

She clenched her inner muscles around me, straining. Sweating.

I rubbed those circles and pushed in, balls deep.

"Ah!" she cried.

"Yes," I panted in a frenzy.

Her eyes rolled back.

I pulsed in and out as she squeezed me hard. I was losing. I was going to—

An enormous shudder quaked her entire body. She might have screamed, but I was coming too, crying out my own ecstasy.

Like an echo, a dying chant faded from my mind. The repeated idea had been loud, but I'd been having sex with this perfect being, so I didn't pay attention. Now, I listened to the echo. It said *mine, mine, mine*.

No, that wasn't right. It said *mate, mate, mate*.

# 8

## JUNIPER

Even I knew better than to wander around the Far Realm without knowing exactly where I was going. The huge island was split into territories riddled with dangers. Yes, I wanted to know, but I wanted to stay alive too.

One territory most people avoided was Sosnakrev. Vampires were a bit like snakes—all calm and glittering and self-possessed until they struck with terrifying speed. That moon energy Luca talked about filled them all the time. It came out as awareness. Or sex, which had been hot and good on the trail.

We held hands as we walked past the enormous black boulder marking the beginning of vampire territory. Well, it wasn't a boulder exactly. More like a crystal or petrified wood. Something precious that probably had deep meaning for the clan beyond marking the border. The stone glimmered in the dying light as though it were made of wet glass. I didn't ask about it. The air held too much tension.

The cold drizzle hadn't let up. Wetness dripped from pine needles high above, falling into our hair. Vampire territory or not, I was eager to get inside out of this chill.

Luca squeezed my hand.

I cast him a look. So many feelings swirled inside me that I would have had no idea how to answer if he asked how I was doing. I was glad to be there, excited to see how vampires lived, and nervous about the ritual and what it would mean for us. Honestly, I needed a hug.

When Luca had taken me against the tree, I sensed his desperation. (I hated to think how edgy I'd be if he hadn't made me come hard.) He didn't say it, but we both knew this trip *mattered*. I just hoped it turned out well for us.

"Let me introduce you," he said softly. I didn't care for the edge in his voice. He kept scanning the mist with that ultra-awareness in his deep-set eyes.

I followed his eyeline but didn't see anyone. "Luca..."

Two shapes materialized in front of us, here as quickly as if they were demi-gods and could walk through the air. The taller one had a craggy, distinguished face that had lost the smoothness of youth. The shorter one, another male, had a long, teardrop-shaped face with blazing eyes. They represented the spectrum of age and appearance I'd personally seen in vampires. They carried no weapons.

Because they were weapons.

Luca tucked his wings tighter against his back and bowed. "Casimir. Dusan."

"Who is this?" asked the older one, his cadence slow and powerful.

I clenched my jaw. Who were these people to Luca? I

wanted to introduce myself, smile, and ask questions, hopefully while they led me to a good meal, but Luca's body language made me stay quiet.

"Casimir"—another bow as he addressed the older vampire —"this is Juniper."

A grunt was the only response. Casimir glowered as he looked me over.

"Juniper, this is Casimir, the leader of our clan." Luca rested his hand on my shoulder.

"Pleased to meet you," I said, resisting the urge to hold out my hand. Casimir didn't look like he'd appreciate that.

"She's smaller than I expected."

I frowned.

"She's a faun," Luca said. His expression mirrored mine. "Why should that matter? You said she would be welcome."

"As a concession to your family, but past this boundary, I cannot guarantee her safety. I will place you in the stag lodge, but the nights get brighter."

That ominous note didn't comfort me. Dusan's labored breathing as he stared at me didn't either.

Luca's eyes flashed. "Juniper is a member of the Assembly of Nyx." He looked like he wanted to say more, but fell quiet. Was a compliment or defense on his lips? Either way, the hope that swelled as he said the words waned faster than the moon when he didn't elaborate.

*Yes, I am a member of the Assembly, so make sure we stay safe.*

When Luca said his family wouldn't agree with my decision to come, I didn't realize the entire clan would scoff at me. I'd worked hard to gain respect and my position. Now, with a mere look, these vampires unraveled my self-assurance like a ball of string.

Luca was naturally a quiet person, but he stood out in any room, at least to me. But next to Casimir and even Dusan, who hadn't spoken, Luca looked young. Normally, I liked his youthfulness—to me, that meant we didn't look quite as mismatched. I loved his smooth face, his lithe body, his vitality. Really, he was nearing thirty, but vampires lived a long time. The contrast now between him and the others made him out to be inexperienced before we'd gotten past introductions.

"All the more reason you shouldn't have brought her," Casimir declared. "But you can't un-move once you've run." As he turned away, his shoulders hitched slightly, like an involuntary muscle twitch.

My body stiffened. No vampire I'd ever met had twitched like that. They moved with icy grace—one of the things I enjoyed watching with Luca—or terrifying speed. I guessed that twitch meant Casimir was losing control. My heartbeat fluttered in my chest. What would happen when the moon was full?

I should have done more to protect myself for this trip. My clothes weren't thick, and vampire fangs measured two segments of my finger when fully extended. I fought for composure.

Luca's eyes fixed on Casimir's back, then slid to the other vampire. Dusan stared at our joined hands a beat longer. Luca glared murderously. The two locked eyes, history coursing between them.

"Don't" was all Luca said.

Dusan's mouth puckered thoughtfully, but he swallowed

any retort he might have said before turning away to join the clan leader on the path.

Luca's shoulders drifted toward his ears, uneasiness in every movement. I tried to catch his eye, but he didn't take the bait.

We followed, passing the glossy stone. My throat felt tight.

I didn't mind a little danger. It was part of the job. But this level of obvious personal hostility was new.

One glance at Luca and his flexed jaw told me how on edge he felt too. I didn't want to bring him down in the eyes of his clan. He deserved care and respect. But I wanted answers too. I wanted him to say more on my behalf. For now, I'd just watch and listen. Later, I'd learn everything.

*Maybe the clan has reasons for feeling the way they do about us. Maybe they just need someone to explain. They'll see us happy together and realize they didn't need to worry.*

As I watched the weathered wings bob from Casimir's muscled back, my thoughts felt naïve, not enlightened.

I stood straighter. If I was going to become the head of the Assembly someday, I couldn't be intimidated by cranky vampires with a bias against other beings.

Past the stone was simply more woods, but with a defined path. "How far is the stag lodge?" I asked.

When no one answered for a few steps, Luca said, "It's just up this path. It's on the edge of the village."

Did Luca's family not want me staying with them? It took all my willpower not to ask more questions, but I figured it was better to get somewhere dry where I could think instead of getting Luca into trouble somehow.

Through the scent of rain, blood and smoke cut in. I wrinkled my nose. We reached a crossroads. The path widened into a semi-paved street up ahead, and branched into smaller tracks right and left.

Casimir and Dusan halted at the crossroads. A beautiful metal object rose in the space where the paths crossed. Flat and circular like a table, its glistening surface had a pole jutting from the middle. When I looked closer, runes and designs in a complicated pattern traced the circumference and spiraled inward. Fluted metal arched from the pole like vampire wings, stretching upward. Atop the wing-like structures was a bubble of the clearest glass I'd ever seen. Some kind of device for mapping the sky? Or merely here as a testament to their craftsmanship?

"The stag lodge is there." Casimir pointed to our right. "Lock the door at night."

Both Casimir and Dusan held their hands in loose fists.

"Welcome back, Luca," he said tersely.

No word for me. Well, then.

Ahead, blocks of black, darker than the trees, peeked through. Buildings, probably. I needed to see more of Sosnakrev, but it looked like that wouldn't happen today.

Luca tipped his head to the clan leader and turned to walk with me.

"Not you. Her." Casimir cracked his knuckles with a quick, almost casual, squeeze of his fist.

My eyebrows lowered.

"What?" Luca asked.

"She stays at the lodge. You come with us."

I couldn't stop a protest from escaping my mouth. "But—"

"Enough concessions have been made already."

Dusan's lips tightened in approval at the leader's words.

I looked at Luca. Here, he needed to vouch for me. These vampires were clearly suspicious of other beings, if not outright hostile. Luca had to bridge that gap before they'd listen to me.

But he said nothing.

A lump formed in my throat. Luca's eyes burned as he stared down the other two vampires, but he didn't protest, didn't insist that we stay together. This trip was supposed to be an intimate experience for *us*. Alone, I was vulnerable. Why didn't he say anything?

"Go on," Casimir urged me.

I cocked my jaw. Plenty of people had tried to push me around, but was this worth fighting about? Releasing a breath, I addressed Luca. "It's fine." The words came out tight. "I'll see you when I can."

Luca's eyes turned liquid sad. His poignant expression reminded me of grief. Not the kind of look I wanted to see right now. "The stag lodge is... interesting," he said. "It's beautiful. I think you'll like it." He squeezed my hand.

The rock in my throat had grown so I couldn't reply. Instead, my fingers slipped from his and I turned to walk down the misty path to find my lodgings alone.

❦  9  ❦

## LUCA

**G**uilt and anger writhed in my head as I watched Juniper pick her way down the path without me. This felt symbolic. Vampires had never fraternized with fauns, never been allowed to mix. In Nyx, I didn't care about that. I shouldn't care here either.

But Casimir was my leader, someone I grew up trusting and obeying. The old ranks slipped into place more easily than I ever would have thought.

My wings stretched half-out, then back in. I could go after Juniper. I could defy Casimir.

I should. My relationship with Juniper was doomed after this trip, no matter how it went, but she deserved protection from me, at least.

"I'm going with her," I declared.

Dusan smiled wickedly.

Ignoring him, I pivoted on my heel and stalked after her.

"Luca!" Casimir called. His voice always carried over every-

63

thing else, even in a crowd, like the voice of tradition or conscience.

I stopped, turned. "It's not right to leave her alone. She's my girlfriend, she's alone in a dangerous place, and I'm staying with her."

"She'll lock the door."

"I *want* to stay with her." If these were the last days I got to spend with Juniper, I damn well wanted to soak up every minute. Why had I hesitated in the first place? Knowing I couldn't spend my life with the mate I loved didn't mean I had to sabotage our relationship early.

Her little form disappearing into the mist broke my heart.

"Not while you're in Sosnakrev." Casimir's gaze turned hard as stone. "Away from our borders, you can engage in behaviors unbefitting to a vampire. You can lower yourself. But while you are here, I insist on dignity and respect."

Rage surged through my body. The moon was waxing, and my instincts grew with it. "Is that what you showed Juniper just now?" I snarled.

Dusan growled back, taking a dangerous step forward. I held my ground. Dusan could mimic Casimir all he wanted, but one day he had to move past that. I'd see to it that *he* would eventually understand Juniper deserved as much respect as anyone else in this village.

Casimir remained icily calm. "Dignity and respect for our kind, yes."

I ground my teeth. "I got written permission for Juniper to participate in the full moon ritual. Nothing is more sacred to us than that. You can't say she's invited to the ritual and then treat her as if she's an outsider."

"I must correct your language," Casimir replied. "She was never invited. She was allowed. And she only has permission to participate in a limited capacity."

The mist against my skin grew clammy. I fished for a salt bead and threw it back. "What do you mean?"

"This is Juniper's first and only time at the ritual. She won't be on the ground with the others. She can't. Even first-time vampires don't begin that way." Casimir strode up the path past the moon dial. I followed, needing answers.

"What do you mean?" I couldn't be separated from Juniper during the ritual. There were so many reasons that was a terrible idea. An orgy while my girlfriend just watched? And I needed some way to protect her. So many vampires fueled by their most primal urges meant that she could be in danger.

Fuck. Why had I agreed to bring her at all?

"I did give you permission to bring her here," Casimir continued, sounding disappointed with himself. "I like you, Luca. You could have been someone." He drew in a deep breath.

I tried to ignore the searing pain in my chest from his words. *I am someone. So is Juniper.*

"Your little faun will be a moon sacrifice."

I stopped short. Sacrifices were tied up on platforms above everyone else. We could approach them, touch them, but not couple with them. Their experience was painful and detached. As a vampire, it was a rite of passage. Hell, I'd done it my first time. But it wasn't the same as being connected with everyone else, letting the moonlight and our bodies meld together in one violent, panting experience of surrender. That was where

Juniper needed to be to understand this part of being a vampire. This part of me.

"That isn't what I meant when I said I wanted her at the ritual," I said.

"It doesn't matter what you wanted." Casimir didn't look at me. "That is all I'm willing to offer. It's more of a concession than I've seen in my lifetime. Frankly, if your family weren't so important to me, I never would have allowed that much."

Juniper, tied up, watching me...

"No."

We reached one of the main streets of Sosnakrev, lined with dark, ornate buildings like jeweled miniatures adopted by the landscape, the perfect blend of art and nature. Polished black stones formed into jaggedly pointed roofs and petrified wood formed multi-storied structures. Tall metal hooks held black and red lanterns that complimented the savage beauty. Juniper would love this. Imagining my home through her eyes gave me a new appreciation and certainty that I needed to bring her here. She was only steps away, alone, at the stag lodge.

"No?" Casimir inquired dangerously. "Another word from you and I'll revoke any kind of permission. Your faun friend will simply have to go home."

Then a thought struck me. "Will all the rules apply to Juniper when she's a sacrifice?"

Dusan's lips parted in surprise, but I kept my attention firmly on Casimir.

"Yes," Casimir answered. "The moon remembers tradition even when we don't." He gave me a flinty look. A warning.

My breath had gone shallow. Only one thing—one declaration—was strong enough to untie a moon sacrifice.

Was I strong enough... or weak enough... to make that declaration to Juniper?

"But it doesn't matter," Casimir went on. "You won't be there."

I halted in the middle of the road.

Dusan turned with a smirk. "I will be."

My gaze shot to our leader. "What the fuck? Casimir, you knew Juniper was coming. I *have* to go with her."

"We never discussed that. It's Dusan's turn."

How had I lost count? Knowing which of us would attend the moon ritual was as normal as remembering to put salt beads in my pocket. Always present. Had my concern for Juniper and our relationship really blinded me to something so obvious?

"I'm going," I declared. "Dusan can have the next two months."

Dusan laughed. "You'd go wild in Nyx without a ritual."

"I have a room," I began, but the protest sounded lame. "We stay safe."

"That's not your decision to make," Casimir said, approaching me with lethal calm. For all his backwards thinking, I had to admire his coolness during all moon phases. He wasn't someone to be easily ruffled. Dusan had the telltale vibration of a vampire about to strike. Casimir's ever-present sternness didn't change much until the ritual itself.

"It is this time." In most things, for Dusan's sake, I'd bow to Casimir's demands. But not now. "Juniper needs me there. I'm going to the clearing whether or not I have permission."

Dusan shot me a withering glance. In it, I saw all our rivalry growing up. The time he ripped my wing so he could win a race. The time he took the two largest bedrooms in our parents' ancestral house (why he needed two, I didn't know.) The time we got in a fight over girl we both liked.

I wasn't always proud of the way I dealt with Dusan, but if he acted like an asshole, he needed to be put in his place. Not just for me, but for Sosnakrev.

"Break one of our sacred laws, and I'll ensure you never set foot here again," said Casimir, his craggy face dangerous.

"How did I know you'd pull something like this?" I snarled at Dusan.

Casimir held out a hand to silence him. "The moon rises and sets when it will. Time, not I, has dictated that this month is Dusan's. At this rate, I might grant him another."

A pang echoed in my chest. "Let him have three after this. But I get this one. Juniper is vulnerable—"

"Which is why it was foolish to bring her!" Casimir shouted.

I stepped up, face to face. The smell of wet leather wafted up between us. "Vampires need to see fauns aren't weak and should be treated with respect." I turned my gaze to Dusan. "*We* are to blame if we're too violent and dangerous to allow others in."

Dusan's shoulders relaxed, the corners of his mouth turning down. For all his tough bluster, part of him wanted to hear me. I could see it.

*Come on.* If he voiced his opinion around Casimir, maybe the leader would listen.

But he said nothing.

"Step down this month, Dusan," I urged. "Just this month."

His chest inflated again and he took a threatening step toward me. "Didn't you hear Casimir? I'm going, and you're not."

I shoved him back. "Bullshit!"

And suddenly, he was on me. Dusan flung me back by my shoulders. No immediate punch to the face. That meant he didn't want to hurt me too much.

I tried to think, but wildness thickened the air so I landed a fist in his gut. Wind gusted out of him. My hand shot up again, this time cracking him in the jaw.

I'd be damned to Abaddon before I'd let Juniper face the moon ritual alone.

"Like children!" yelled a voice like a whip crack.

It was enough to pierce the haze in my mind. I wrenched myself away from Dusan, who was rubbing his chin where I'd hit him.

Casimir glowered at us. "Like children! I'm ashamed of you both! Dusan goes. You stay."

Dusan started to smile, but Casimir whirled on him. "You are one monumentally stupid choice away from losing that right. Based on what I've seen today, there's a good chance you might. So, go!"

At the snapped word, Dusan obeyed, regret settling over him almost visibly. He was hotheaded and stupid, but his heart wasn't bad. Just slow, sometimes.

I watched him walk through the mist, like I'd watched Juniper, furious with myself. I should have said more to Dusan. I should have fought harder for Juniper.

"Please," I began again.

"Enough," Casimir bit out. "Your lack of forethought does not constitute the necessity that I change everyone else's plans. Especially now." He sighed. "Luca..."

He rarely was at a loss for words. At least his expression spoke volumes. He wished I had turned out better.

It was hard not to respond to that look. I turned out fine. Just because I didn't follow the traditional vampire path for my life didn't mean I'd made a mistake. Juniper would never be a mistake.

*Moon sacrifice.*

*Dusan is attending instead of you.*

For a second, I wanted to run back to the stag lodge and take Juniper home. But that would mean traveling on the road during the full moon. No time to get safely to one of the inn's demon rooms.

My lips peeled back from my teeth as I met the clan leader's eyes.

Trapped. I was trapped. Any hope I had of making this experience a good one for my relationship with Juniper died.

Tonight, I'd try to figure out what to do, but all I could see were more walls closing in around us.

❧ 10 ❧

# JUNIPER

aybe this was how the vampires felt with the full moon approaching. In my belly was a mass of emotions. Heartbreak, irritation, wonder.

The stag lodge was more than just pretty. It was magnificent. Hard to believe I had it all to myself. Casimir, the leader of Luca's clan, had instructed me to lock the door, so I did as soon as I stepped inside. Still, I felt like another vampire could step around the corner any second. The interior was dark, almost black, with thick curtains over the two windows and red candles spiking up through elaborate candelabras. Blood-red rugs made the space more cozy and less forbidding. Dark dark dark. That made sense. Vampires disliked sunlight, although I hadn't realized to what extent. Come to think of it, Dusan's eyes looked slightly puffy, as if he wasn't used to being awake at this time. At home, overcast skies were enough to make Luca happy, and the Far Realm was often stormy. I wrestled a pad and writing tool from my luggage.

*Black curtains. Wide spaces between furniture. Dark. Red candles.*

Luca and I could get black curtains when we got home so they could block the light more completely when it got too bright outside.

The pad of paper drooped in my hands, and I tapped the floor impatiently with my hoof. The rug swallowed the clicking sound I expected.

Why hadn't Luca insisted on coming with me? When he had to choose between me and Casimir, he sided with the powerful vampire clan leader. Casimir had been the clan leader for Luca's whole life, but Casimir also treated me like trash. If he was ever going to change his mind about me, he needed to understand my value. That started with education—the kind of thing I was constantly trying to do in Nyx. Luca's inaction felt like betrayal.

Probably because it was. I wasn't somebody to just throw aside, to treat as less important. My entire life's work was to show that everyone was important. Even small fauns could take leadership roles in the biggest city in the Far Realm.

Except now, I felt just how small I was.

This trip was for Luca to reconnect with his roots and for me to learn about them. How could I do that if I was stuffed into this out of the way building?

Doubts about our relationship surged like an angry sea. I didn't want to think this way. I loved Luca. He needed to prove that he loved me too, but so far...

I dashed away a tear with an angry hand and lugged my things into the nearest hallway, searching for a bed. This building was probably four times the size of the little house I shared with Luca. Did I really have it all to myself? The heavy curtains and flickering light made it hard to see if I was really alone.

"Hello?" I called. "Hello?"

No answer.

Through an open door, I spotted a large, four-poster bed with dark gray sheets. "Hello?" I tried one more time.

When nobody responded, I flung my stuff on the floor of the bedroom. The bed was huge for only one person.

The skin on my arms felt chilly and damp from the mist outside. Visions of Luca pinning me to that tree, wings outspread, sent a jolt of desire between my legs. He should be here to sleep in this bed with me. Or not sleep. Or talk.

The ritual would be here in the blink of an eye. Time to see Sosnakrev was running out, and I wanted my best friend here to show me around, introduce me to his culture.

Instead, all I got was this. Was I just supposed to wait here in these dark, elaborate quarters until someone came to fetch me?

In that instant, I knew two things.

One, I'd learn everything I could about vampire lifestyle and culture from the stag lodge. The smallest things could teach a lot if you were looking.

Two, no one could treat a member of the Assembly like a misbehaving child. With or without Luca, despite the vampires who didn't want me in their village, I'd leave to have a look around.

I'D BE CAREFUL.

Wrapping a thick scarf around my neck to fend off the chilly drizzle, I undid the latch, opened the door, and peeked outside. The stag lodge was breathtaking, actually, but I didn't come here to sit in one place until called for. I'd simply see the town and then I'd come back. Easy. Casimir wouldn't find me, I wouldn't disturb any moon-riled vampires, and even Luca wouldn't know that I had left.

Sourness pooled in my stomach. Luca should have stood up for me.

I left my bag in the sumptuous dark room in the lodge, but took my pad for notes. I'd already written pages while investigating every corner of the stag lodge. Now I was ready to see the village.

Outside, the sun had already set. Flickering in the light of the sparce lanterns, lashes of drizzling rain fell. It looked ready to turn to snow when the temperature dropped far enough.

Fighting off a shiver, I squinted into the dark. There was the object marking the crossroads. In the blackness, it looked like the frozen figure of a vampire with wings outstretched. My head knew it wasn't really a person, but my heartbeat kicked up all the same. Clever. They probably wanted it to look like that at night. I breathed slowly, forcing myself to calm down as I got closer to it before taking the path to the right.

No movement.

No trick of the eye.

Tomorrow, the moon would be full. Self-control would snap, and I'd become prey in the eyes of the vampires surrounding me here.

Maybe this was a bad idea. Casimir had led this clan for a long time. His shortness with me might have just been his brand trying to keep me safe. Still, no need to be rude about it.

My thoughts strayed again to Luca. Besides seeing the town and learning about vampire culture, this trip was supposed to bring me closer to him. The ritual performed here in his hometown was the last piece of his heart I'd never seen. And I wanted all of him. Was that selfish? Right now, I felt like an intruder, as if I'd forced my way in. He wanted me here too, right?

I swallowed the lump of doubt in my throat and paced forward through the mud. The sharp smell of snowfall tinged the air. Soon, this path would become ice as winter set in.

Then the trees parted to reveal a clearing littered with buildings. I sucked in a breath.

Sosnakrev.

The wetness in the air obscured my view, but I could still make out soaring black structures slick with rain. Several were as high as the trees, with no windows in the higher levels. Faun dwellings were all single story, but these pointed up like shards of black glass. That brutal, elegant style reminded me of a miniature of Hades' castle I'd seen once in a room of curiosities set up by devout kelpies. Did vampires live on each level of these buildings, or was the structure open inside, allowing them to spread their wings and fly around?

My hand strayed to my pocket, then back to my side. Ideas and curiosity burned through me like ale. But I couldn't take my notepad out in this weather. I'd have to get somewhere dry first.

A shadow moved in the corner of my eye.

I swiveled to look at it.

Two shadows. Vampires.

Quietly, I stepped backward into tree cover, hopefully out of sight.

Of course vampires would be out at night. Luca usually worked during the day to match my schedule, but he cooked indoors and didn't have to be out in the sun. His eyes and skin were sensitive to bright light. Here, everyone could simply adjust their schedules to spend most of their waking hours at night. I should have expected this.

A swift glance upward only confirmed what I already knew. The moon hung round and blinding bright above the trees.

Where was Luca? The moon always made me think of him. Yes, he had angry outbursts when the moon neared the full, but he also got more aggressive during sex, which I liked, despite the bruises I had to cover up afterward.

With these two strangers, though, a nearly full moon could mean more random aggression from them too. What would they do if they saw a strange faun wandering around?

My belly tightened. I was fast but not very strong. Definitely smaller than vampires.

The two shadows got close enough that I could see their features. Dusan and someone I didn't know. I bent down so a line of younger trees blocked me partially from view. These pines had too-skinny trunks. I gripped the fabric of my outfit to channel my nerves.

But I wasn't ready to return to the stag lodge yet. I'd gotten only one tantalizing glance at Sosnakrev. As my eyes adjusted, more figures appeared farther away. The village bustled with movement, but Dusan and the stranger walked closest to me.

Slowing my heavy breathing, I listened. The two were talking.

"...get back from the hunt?" said the stranger.

"I haven't seen him," Dusan replied.

"He'd better hurry. I love slow roasted meat."

"We have plenty for the feast."

"It's not enough."

"What do you know?"

A growl. "I know I have an appetite to eat a whole deer myself."

My stomach turned. Fauns and deer weren't related, but the similarity in some of our anatomy made them almost every faun's favorite animal. We'd never eat one. It would have been like a human eating their beloved dog.

"Don't worry. You can fill yourself up before the ritual. Don't be an ass." A sullen note entered Dusan's tone.

"Poor Dusan," the other mocked. "Sad that you're related to a blood traitor? Or maybe you can't wait to fuck your brother's little hoofer."

I gasped before I could stifle it. First the word *brother* and then the word *hoofer*. That was a term I hadn't heard in years. I turned raging hot and my fingers curled into fists. I had half a mind to march out and punch that vampire in the nose. Surely, I could get one swift hit to his face before they'd stop me...?

But Dusan beat me to it.

The other vampire, who was bigger than Dusan, stumbled backward, obviously caught off guard by Dusan's attack. "Fuck you!" he yelled and barreled forward.

They became a flurry of wings and limbs, smashing to the ground. The thick sound of knuckles against flesh sounded through the square. Moonlight glinted on fangs. Why weren't the others rushing to stop this?

I definitely wouldn't. As a rule, I was against violence, but not even a twinge of guilt touched me as I watched them. Hopefully Dusan would knock the other senseless.

A ripping noise shredded through the air. It was Dusan's shirt. The other vampire held the ragged end of the shirt in his fist. But it hadn't ripped through. Snatching the other half, he tore the shirt in half.

An uncomfortable jolt ran through me. They were still fighting, but... was that all they were doing?

"Enough!"

I jumped. Casimir stalked in from my left, all muscle and wings. His craggy face looked exactly the same as it had a few hours ago. Maybe he was disappointed in everyone, not only intruders like me.

"Enough!" He hauled Dusan off the other vampire. Their clothes were half on, and they both breathed hard through gritted teeth.

"Dusan, you know better," Casimir snarled. "Go home. Tell Luca the ritual is his tomorrow."

Dusan showed his teeth reflexively, but he shook himself, jerked his head into a bow, and stalked away.

Casimir turned his attention to the other, the one who had started it with those vile words. "Bogdan. What did you do?"

My skin shivered at the dark command in Casimir's voice.

Bogdan scoffed. "Nothing."

"Bullshit!" Casimir cut him off. "Dusan wouldn't attack you for no reason."

Bogdan revised his stance. Maybe a few seconds to cool off made him realize that he was facing the leader of the clan and needed to relax. "Dusan's worked up over nothing. He's angry and he took it out on me."

"I will not stand violence in my streets." Casimir almost seemed to grow, his wings spiky at the top. "If you can't control yourself, I rescind the ritual."

Bogdan's mouth fell open. "But you'll let that little hoofer in?"

There it was again.

"Shut your mouth," Casimir snapped, his wings flexing dangerously. "She is Luca's guest. I harbor enough respect for him to extend to her."

I pursed my lips.

"So you will not use such language here. You said something like that to Dusan?"

Bogdan shrugged.

"Moon-cursed cretin," Casimir muttered to himself. "You will not be allowed near her or anyone else performing the ritual tomorrow night."

I released a breath. I couldn't stand the idea of going to a ritual with a person like Bogdan. Thank goodness Casimir had intervened, even if his defense of me wasn't all one could wish for.

After a couple more minutes, Casimir convinced Bogdan to go home too. The spot where violence had erupted a minute ago lay quiet and empty in front of me. In the distance, I could hear more voices, but the indistinct words didn't sound confrontational.

Still, I didn't move from my hiding spot for a while. No one had seen me. But, during the fight, I had felt so vulnerable. These strong, winged vampires attacking each other... If they had turned their attention to me, what would have happened?

*But it didn't. Nothing happened.*

Nothing but learning that Dusan was Luca's brother. I knew he had a brother he didn't talk much about, but, really? Luca couldn't tell me when Casimir and Dusan met us at the border?

I ground my teeth. Luca knew about all my siblings. I'd told him a ton about my family, except a little faun-specific stuff that I didn't think he'd relate to. Should I have explained all that too?

My mind was a whirlwind and my body a misty, freezing mess. My skin felt feverish—hot with rage then chilled with wet cold. I still wanted to see more of Sosnakrev, but, more than anything, I needed to find my boyfriend.

Right now.

✤  II  ✤

# JUNIPER

**M**ore voices rose the longer I stayed in my hiding place. The streets in front of the slick black buildings began filling up with more moving figures. Judging from my experience with Dusan and Bogdan, I didn't want to run into any of them.

I flicked moisture off my clothes, taking steadying breaths of pine-scented air. Was Sosnakrev turning me into a timid faun? I vowed I'd never be timid or assume the worst about others, like my parents did. I wanted to be part of healing misconceptions, not supporting them.

Then why was I so scared? I'd searched for lycans on my own, for gods' sake. But wolf beasts were more predictable than vampires near the full moon.

Or boyfriends who acted like they didn't want you to know anything about them.

*You'd think two years would be enough time to know someone...*

Dusan was Luca's brother, and I hadn't known about it. Luca had to have a good reason. Granted, we both held some things back about our families, but this seemed like a pretty big thing to hide. And why?

Tomorrow was feeling more and more like the tipping point. Would we survive this ritual, or would it break us?

It was almost laughable how worried I was about emerging from my hiding spot when, in just a few hours, I'd be totally naked in a big group of them.

I cleared my throat, trying to clear my mind with it, and finally moved.

Casimir had told me not to leave the stag lodge, so I had to avoid running into him if I could help it. Without help, though, I doubted I could find Luca.

After his fight with Bogdan, Dusan had walked that way, roughly up and to the left. I'd start there. Maybe the two of them were staying together, since Luca wasn't with me.

Striding forward with more confidence than I felt, I approached a group of three female vampires in front of one of the biggest buildings. Two were cleaning large buckets and the third chatted with them, tying up little scraps of cloth with lightning-quick fingers. I couldn't see what she put inside each one.

"Hello," I greeted.

All three turned long, pale faces toward me. None of them had Luca's expressiveness, so it was like looking at a wall of masks.

"Hi, I'm... looking for Luca. Do you know where I can find him?"

The one with the tied-up cloth broke into a fanged smile. "You must be Juniper."

I wasn't sure whether to feel relieved or worried. "Yes," I admitted.

"My name is Viviana." She set her latest parcel to the side and pushed her hair behind her ear. It was such a familiar gesture that it strangely put me at ease. "So, you and Luca..."

"He's my boyfriend."

One of the people cleaning buckets raised an eyebrow.

"A vampire and a faun," said Viviana. "I think it's romantic." She reached out and touched my arm while shooting a look at the other two.

"It is," I confirmed. So few people had that reaction when they learned about us that I felt touched. I still loved Luca, even though I was furious. "Thank you, Viviana. I'm glad he let me come."

"We're glad too. So, you're coming to the full moon ritual, I'm told."

I fought not to squirm. "Yes, I am. It's part of Luca's heritage, so I asked to be a part of it."

The three women shared knowing looks.

"Outsiders don't get in," said one washing a bucket. I couldn't read her tone, and I was usually pretty good at doing that. Her eyes blazed into mine. Was that anger? Amazement? Lust?

"Here," Viviana said, saving me from responding by handing me one of her expertly tied little bags. Through the silky fabric, I could feel something hard and round, no bigger than a tooth. "We all get them."

Oh...

"Don't they hand these out before we... go in?"

Viviana smiled. Vampires were all so beautiful. "Yes. If you'd rather wait."

A thought struck me. "Am I going in through the same entrance as everybody else?"

Viviana tilted her head, a gesture similar to what Luca did when he wasn't sure how to answer. "There are only rumors. I'm not sure."

I bit my lip, closing my hand over the little bag. "I'll just keep it, in case."

Viviana nodded toward the package. "Take it now or later, as long as it's before the drums." She gave me another intoxicating smile.

The two other women listening to our conversation kept scrubbing the buckets. Memories of what Luca told me flooded back. Those buckets... Were they for the blood? They were deep enough that the vampires had to reach almost their entire arm inside.

I swallowed thickly.

Viviana flicked her eyes to the side. "I think Luca is staying in there." She knotted another bag. "You look cold."

"Or you could stay with us," purred another, but her eyes darkened right away, apparently sensing her bad timing.

Viviana went so still, I felt like prey in the sights of a predator about to go in for the kill. I was too close. She could grab my arm and pull me in.

I put on a smile. "No, thank you. I'll just say goodnight to Luca."

No one reached for me, although their volatility hung heavily in the air as I walked away. I couldn't explain the feeling, but turning my back seemed like a bad idea. In a village of vampires, though, it was impossible to avoid doing that. I picked up my pace.

Viviana had indicated the building next door, so I made my way toward it. My hooves sank into the muddy street. I didn't think I'd be overwhelmed when I got here—nervous, maybe— but now, holding this medicine, looking at the buckets, watching the fight, shivering in the cold, all while Luca let me stay alone the night before a dangerous orgy? I was more upset than I could remember being since I was little. Add to that the revelation that Dusan was Luca's brother, and by the time I knocked on the door, I didn't care if Casimir answered it, looming over me. I didn't care that it was cold. I didn't care that Luca would be able to read my face immediately.

I was livid.

The black door, made of metal or maybe petrified wood, had ancient symbols on it. So much I didn't know, didn't understand, and couldn't take in fast enough to fit what I already knew of vampires. Each symbol felt like a new secret Luca had kept from me. This damn place found every soft spot I had and shook its head at how small and naïve I was to come at all.

Orange light poured out as the door opened to reveal a waistcoat-covered chest. I looked up.

Dusan. In the dim light of what looked like a cavernous room inside, Dusan's injuries stood out. The pale skin around his glaring eyes was purpling.

"I need to see Luca."

"Not now," Dusan growled, annoyance painted over his face.

He expected to see Casimir standing here. That was the reason he whipped open the door so quickly.

Adrenaline propelled me onward. "Yes now."

"Casimir said—"

"I don't care what he said." Then I realized what I sounded like. "I do care what he says. But it's important that I see Luca right now."

He blinked slowly at me. I couldn't tell if he was mocking, or thinking, or just slow. It was better than the unpredictable violence I sensed at other times.

"Please," I added.

He sighed a curse through gritted teeth. "Be quick."

"Okay. Yes, I will." I kicked mud off my hooves and hurried inside.

It smelled like salt in here. It smelled like *him.* The entry room was twice as high as the main room in the stag lodge, with blood-red curtains hanging from the ceiling, a similar style to what I'd seen before. There was a telescope by one curtained window and an arrangement of low, backless couches in the center of the room. Above the fireplace hung four family portraits—two I recognized as Luca and Dusan. My heart didn't know what to do with that painting. It felt like Luca belonged here at least as much as he belonged in our little house in Nyx. Here, he was important.

How well did I even know Luca? Had I fallen in love with a fantasy instead of a person?

"Jun, is everything all right?"

I lowered my eyes from the high portraits to find Luca, dark hair mussed with bathwater, wings flaring up, wearing a black silk robe open at the neck, emerging from a farther room. A crease formed between his eyebrows and his eyes flashed through too many emotions to sift through. Happiness at seeing me only lasted for the blink of an eye. In another second, his gaze shifted from me to his brother.

"No, it's not," I said, my rage rushing back.

His eyes flashed with concern and anger. "What's wrong? Were you out on the streets by yourself?" Extending a hand, he moved toward me.

I stepped back, closer to Dusan. The danger I felt coming from him wasn't as poisonous as the pain and betrayal I felt from Luca. "Are you going to say I'm not allowed?" I could practically hear my molars grinding together.

"No! No, you can do whatever you want." He popped more than one salt bead from his pocket into his mouth, a sure sign that he was trying not to let the moon get the best of his emotions. "I didn't want it to be like this. I'm sorry you have to stay—"

"Are you? You didn't say anything. It's not like we don't talk to each other, Luca, and you didn't tell me anything!"

His cheeks moved as he sucked the salt beads. "What do you mean?"

I cast a pointed look at the portraits.

He followed my gaze, chest blushing. "I had a good reason. And it's not like it was a secret, exactly."

"What would you call it, then?" I scoffed.

His deep eyes returned to mine. "There are... some other things I need to tell you too." The way he said it made my skin tingle with dread. "Let's sit down."

"I want to stand," I said, crossing my arms. The new movement made me shiver all over again.

He clearly spotted the small parcel in my hand but said nothing about it. Instead, he made an offer I could never refuse. "I have blankets and mulled wine."

Against my will, something in me melted. I deserved to be comfortable during this conversation. Scowling, I let Luca indicate one of the low, red couches. He opened a black chest hidden behind a door and drew out thick, velvety blankets.

I greedily grabbed for them and made a cocoon for myself, crossing my legs so they fit inside. While I got cozy, Luca went deeper into the house to pour the wine.

At some point, Dusan must have retreated, because I didn't see him, and the room was large and open enough to spot him if he'd stayed.

Luca settled beside me, lowering the cushion, his

comforting weight tempting me to lean into it as he offered me a steaming mug of mulled wine.

I gripped the blankets harder and held them to me like a shield.

"You'll like it," he coaxed, holding the steam under my nose.

The cinnamony smell was too much. I snaked one of my arms out of my blanket pod to take the mug. Its fired clay design was just like the mugs at home, and, for once, I was glad I had nothing new to learn about.

Which reminded me...

I took a fortifying sip. I shouldn't have been surprised, but the taste was saltier than I preferred. "Luca, you didn't tell me about your family."

He didn't deny it. Instead, he stared levelly back at me, his gaze lingering on the wetness coating my lips. Now wasn't the time for any of that, although my body automatically warmed at that look and the peek at his chest that the black robe revealed. Stupid body.

Could we really have this conversation the day before the full moon? This was around the time he would lock himself in one of the rooms at the inn in preparation for the vampire wildness to take him.

"Dusan," I charged on. "He's your brother."

Luca released a breath, his eyes softening with truth. He tucked his wings closer around himself. Their membranous edges touched my heap of blankets. "Yes, he is. I..." His eyes darted, as if he was trying to find an explanation, or maybe another lie.

I took an angry gulp of wine, this time with the medicine

Viviana had given me. "I thought we trusted each other, Luca. I thought we told each other things. And now I find out that Dusan is your brother? You didn't even tell me when he showed up with Casimir at the entrance!"

At the mention of Casimir, Luca flexed his sharp jaw.

The longer he stayed silent, the more painful the ache in my chest grew. I thought the last piece of him was buried here in his home, at the ritual. I'd never seen him participate in the orgy that marked his cultural community. But as I watched him now, it was like I couldn't see past his expressive eyes at all. What was he thinking? Did he love me? Had he been lying about everything?

The pain turned into a watery rage. "Say something, Luca!"

"I'm thinking, Juniper," he snapped, then wilted. "I'm sorry. I'm sorry." He stroked the back of the pile of blankets, but I stiffened at even that touch. "I wanted to tell you about Dusan."

"Then why didn't you?"

The look he gave me lodged a lump in my throat. It was unlike any look I'd seen from him in the two years we'd been together. Tears lined his bottom lids. It was as if his eyes got bigger, glossier. I could see myself in them. His brow furrowed, and small, dimpled lines spread from one side of his mouth. I could read each piece, but not the whole. His sensuous mouth apologized, his forehead showed intensity, his eyes devastation. All together, it felt like... a goodbye.

My vision blurred. I fought the urge to grab for him.

"Why didn't you?" I asked again, choking on the words.

"I should have, but you're so kind that I... didn't."

Anger simmered under my skin again. "What does that mean?"

"He's in line for clan leader."

I struggled to put the pieces together. Why did that—?

"Casimir doesn't have any children of his own, so he chose our family to succeed him a long time ago. Dusan is the oldest, so he's in line to lead."

"Why wouldn't you tell me that?" I demanded.

"Because you'd want to come here."

I recoiled. "What's wrong with that? I'm here now." *Against Casimir's orders...* Was that where Dusan had gone, to tell him? Maybe I was still safe, since their last interaction had been so confrontational.

Luca let out a frustrated breath. "You'd want to *stay* here, or let me stay here. I'm... I was supposed to help Dusan with the clan." He lowered his eyes before bringing them up again to meet mine. Moisture leaked from his hair onto his temples.

"You... gave up the leadership of your people to be with me?" My chest felt frozen. I took another drink. Was I flattered? Angry?

Both. Definitely both.

"Dusan can handle it."

My mind jumped to the fight Dusan had had in the street. Luca knew about that, right?

"Why would you do that?" I asked.

"I didn't tell you because you'd feel pressured to make me come back," he said, answering the wrong part of my question. "You'd do the right thing. But I..."

My heart jumped. Would he say *those words*? Would he admit he felt the same way about me that I did about him? I squeezed the mug in my hands, but the blankets hid my trembling.

"You have your work in Nyx," he said, fluttering his wings once before tucking them in again. This evasiveness was maddening. "The Assembly needs you. You're so godsdamned necessary to them. I'd hate for you to throw that away just for me. I won't let you."

I let the blankets drop so they pooled around my waist. Setting down my mug, I raised myself up so I matched his height on the couch. "You didn't think I could make my own decision? You didn't even give me the chance! How necessary could I be to the Assembly if I'd abandon it at a moment's notice?"

"Wouldn't you?" he challenged, leaning closer.

"No!"

"You'd tell me to break things off and go back to my people."

I considered. "Yes."

He cocked his jaw.

"I didn't want to go back, I didn't want to break things off, but I would have done it if you told me to. I couldn't risk it."

My skin felt too hot with a hundred emotions, so I wound off my scarf and dropped it on the ground.

The thick certainty that there were too many differences, too many obstacles between us, slowed my blood. Was there no way Luca and I could stay together? Did I even want a lifetime together after this? Perfect mates didn't have to deal with so much friction, did they?

"Should I leave?" The quiet question felt like it was wrenched out of my chest. The moon ritual wouldn't fill in all the gaps and lies about Luca. It wouldn't magically make him love me more. If anything, this trip strained our relationship instead of healing it.

"No!" He let out a dry chuckle. "I literally fought Dusan for the right to go with you to the ritual tomorrow."

Family members. I hadn't put that together. "*He* was going to go to the ritual instead of you?"

"He asked Casimir weeks ago, but no one told me until I arrived."

I breathed a curse. "Thank Hades Dusan got into a fight tonight, then. Casimir said he was banned this time."

"He's pissed, yeah." Luca's face softened into something I recognized. He was the only vampire I'd seen tonight who looked ready for bed. A reminder that he and I had the same rhythms, the same life. He looked warm. That simple observation made me want to get closer. He continued, "You saw that? He's not as bad as he seems. Most of the time, anyway. This moon cycle has fucked with him. At least this time it paid off so I could go with you tomorrow."

"I thought you'd arranged everything with Casimir in advance," I said in a small voice.

"I got permission for you to participate. I guess I just assumed..." He shrugged and threw two more salt beads into his mouth. He was sucking them at twice the rate I normally witnessed. "And there's one more thing."

I sat back on my knees, blood running cool. The soft blankets under my legs and dangerous beauty of Luca's ancestral home contrasted with my rising panic. "What?"

Luca avoided my eyes. "I argued with Casimir about it, but I had to stop before I got aggressive with him. Believe me, Jun. I tried." He ran a hand through his wet hair. "He said that, because this is your first time, you have to be a moon sacrifice."

I scrunched my eyebrows. "On the platform?"

Amusement crossed his features, as if he was proud I remembered. But, of course I remembered the details of the moon ritual. Not only was it a nerve-racking, exclusive event I was participating in, but it was part of him. "Yes." His amusement faded. "Above everything."

My pulse jogged faster. "Will you be up there too?" I knew the answer as soon as I asked.

Luca swallowed visibly. "Not the whole time. We can... visit moon sacrifices, but they don't fully participate." As if he couldn't stop himself, he looked down and bared his fangs.

"I won't be down with the rest of you?"

"And you can't be entered."

*Entered.* No sex for the sacrifices. "So, I'm just supposed to watch? You want me to watch you having sex with a bunch of other people?"

"You think I want that?" he snapped.

"I don't know what you want anymore! Maybe you want to be done."

"I want…!" But he clenched his jaw and didn't finish the sentence. I watched as he took ten deep, slow breaths, his hands in fists.

This had to be hard for him. Whatever Luca had done by not telling me about his family, we had meant a lot to each other for years. He didn't love me—not like I loved him. Fine. He still cared about me and his people. And here I was poking at him with pointed words.

I wrapped my mouth around half a dozen apologies, trying out words that fit. Instead, I said, "I'll be the moon sacrifice. It's all right." Resisting Casimir's rule, which sounded reasonable according to their customs, would only hurt Luca and Dusan, who bore the weight of the clan on their shoulders.

Luca pursed his mouth, which I knew was salt flavored. I licked my lips. "It's not all right. You should get the full experience. Hell, I should get the full experience. If I know you're here and I have to engage with everyone *but* you, what kind of ritual is that?" He blinked rapidly, as if waking up or realizing he'd said too much.

The image of Viviana and the other female vampires I

talked to came to mind. Luca would have no shortage of willing partners. Even in Nyx, people flirted with Luca on the street before understanding that, bafflingly, he was with me.

"It's all right," I repeated. "I won't blame you for anything. You know I won't. I'll learn a lot up there."

"It will be safer," he mused, but his expression darkened like he was ready for a fight.

I remembered Dusan's altercation in the street. "It gets pretty violent down there, doesn't it? When I saw Dusan..."

He laughed. "Oh, he's unhinged sometimes. You'd still rather have sex with me than him, right?"

I hit Luca's hard shoulder. "I'm not ready to joke. You lied to me. And you should be here in Sosnakrev. Why give up everything just to be with me in Nyx?" I realized what I was saying as it came out of my mouth. "They don't give you enough respect there. You could do some good here." With me doing research for helpful policies there and Luca fighting to undermine prejudices here, we could both be proud of our contributions to the Far Realm.

But he was glaring at me. I'd only seen that look around the full moon. Normally, he was so sensitive and kind, but something had shifted. Against my will, my gut somersaulted. Not with fear—never fear—but lust. Luca so rarely let himself go. "Dusan's got it," he growled. "I'm not moving back here."

"Think about it, at least."

The answering curl of his lip pooled warmth in my lower belly. I was only desperate for him because I was losing him. That had to be it. I couldn't lose him, and I couldn't keep him. The tension sped up my breath.

"This was a bad idea," he said, low. "We shouldn't have

come. All the fucking vampires around here think you're too little, like you're naïve, like you're easy prey. And I just don't know what to do." He gestured behind me to the hallway. "I washed up just to get my thoughts straight, but then I was tired at the wrong time and kept picturing you up in the air, or with us." He barely made sense, his words hurried and breathless. "And the idea of all their hands on you…"

My neck flushed and he grabbed it.

"All of them prodding and touching and fucking you. I want to fight them all, and…" He paused to catch his breath. His irises had disappeared into black. "And I want to watch." Moon energy snapped his restraints. He released my throat and dragged me so I sat sideways on the couch, legs on either side of his hips. The blanket lay in a heap behind me as I faced him. "Because when they taste this pretty cunt"—he jabbed his fingers into my wet heat and ruthlessly stroked—"they won't be able to get enough. They'll need more. They'll envy us."

I gasped and writhed as his fingers moved and he rose up to loom over me, a pale face against dark walls. He forced me to lean all the way back until my back hit the couch.

"They'll understand." A savage smile split his face like a predator looking at dinner. "Knees up."

I obeyed, bending them and tucking them against my chest. He leaned his weight on my legs, dominating my body, and fumbled with himself. He growled as if he couldn't get himself out fast enough. He was already so hard. My head fell back as he thrust inside me, painful and deep.

"Ah," he breathed, crushing his body against mine. "They won't be able to let you go. Can you take it? Can you take us all?"

I whimpered, nodding. His pace increased and his hands grew more insistent, pinching my side and fisting my hair. He brought my face right up to his. I panted, and he seemed to drink my breath.

"With the moon looking on. And bodies all around. And they're thrusting inside you." His fierce, heavy thrusts matched his frenzied words.

My hold on sense was slipping. He bared his teeth as he locked eyes with me. Any time I grunted or jerked or sighed, his pupils grew wider and his grip on my hair tightened.

Luca was already good at chasing my orgasm, but when the moon affected him, he undid me. We'd never had sex the night before the full moon. It was too dangerous, he said.

But I loved it. Loved him. And I was losing him and I wanted to hold him even harder and not let go.

I dug my nails into his back, slipping my fingers into the slit the robe had for his wings so I could touch his bare skin.

He groaned my name. In response, my fingers curled, digging deeper. I wanted to hurt him a little bit, like he'd hurt me. Like he'd lied to me. I broke the skin.

His eyes squeezed shut, then flared open, wild. Without warning, he pulled out, flipped me over, and angled up my hips. His speed and strength knocked the air from my lungs. Now my cheek and fists pressed against the soft blanket, while my ass touched bare flesh. I twisted to look at him. He'd stripped off his robe and kneeled behind me. The divot between his abs already glistened with sweat in the low light.

"Bad girl," he whispered. And he drove in again, this time even deeper. My cheek slid across the blankets as he ground relentlessly against me. Once I could open my eyes and close my mouth from the overflow of hot, sweet sensation, my eyes landed on the other couches and the open doorway.

Dusan stood watching us, his chest rising and falling heavily as he gripped the doorframe with one hand so hard I saw a crack under his fingers.

I gasped and pushed up on all fours. "Luca!"

But he didn't stop. If anything, his frantic plunging grew more intense. His skin smacked against mine, echoing in the quiet air. I bobbed forward and backward with each of his delicious movements.

Dusan hadn't looked away. Instead, he was staring at me.

I'd never been watched like this before. Based on Luca's grunts and moans, an audience didn't lessen his lust either. As I stared back into Dusan's eyes, the tiny part of me that was still lucid tried to figure out how I felt about this. Was I okay being watched by Luca's brother?

Luca grabbed a handful of my generous hip and jammed me back into him.

Dusan blinked, almost a wince.

"Harder," I breathed. "Faster."

Luca obeyed, fucking me like a jackrabbit. The tips of his protracted wings entered my peripheral vision, so I knew he was close.

Having someone watch Luca take me so violently like this, marking me as his, was... thrilling. Justifying, almost. *See, our bodies were made for each other.*

Only they weren't.

"Slow down," I gasped. "Not yet." But I was gripping the blankets in trembling fists and mewling high-pitched breaths.

This couldn't be the last time it was just the two of us. It couldn't. We had to hold on.

Luca couldn't respond. He was already coming inside me with a roar. If I hadn't been wearing my dress, his fingers would have broken skin. As his warmth filled me, I touched myself to push myself over the edge with him.

When my walls squeezed around him, Luca released an unholy sound that mingled with my ragged cry.

Drained, I fluttered open my eyes. I was lying on my side, cradled in Luca's arms. His chest pressed against my back and his bare leg slung over mine. I was still clothed. Despite the layers between us, I already felt Luca getting hard again.

That was fast.

I glanced up toward the doorway. Dusan was gone.

Luca's tongue pressed against the back of my neck. "Mmm, your sweat," he murmured. "Right here."

We had a routine of Luca licking the sweat off me after sex, even when the moon's energy wasn't a factor. Now, though, he wasn't licking. His tongue stayed pressed against my pulse. I could tell he hadn't broken the skin, but something about this suspended position told me he was fighting the urge.

How much danger was I in? Luca had never let me see him in this state. I knew most of the rumors about vampires were harmful nonsense, but Luca had admitted to me himself that he'd love nothing more than tasting my blood. Since it wasn't safe, he wouldn't do it. But he said he knew it would taste delicious.

I lay still, my heartbeat kicking up.

Luca growled against my skin, kissing the spot. "Perfect."

"Your brother was here," I whispered.

"Did that bother you?" He continued slowly licking and kissing my neck.

"No. I liked him knowing I was yours."

"Dirty." The word reverberated through my chest. "He'll never know how perfect you are, how you slide against my cock, and how every little noise and touch drives me crazy. And how you taste like the richest blood." He ran his tongue from my shoulder to my chin. I leaned into the sensation.

A vampire and a faun. Everyone said it couldn't work.

And, it turned out, despite all my fighting and all the love I had for Luca, it probably couldn't.

He couldn't see my face, so I let tears fill up my eyes, squeezing them shut in a silent sob.

I forced myself to stay awake after I helped Juniper sneak back to the stag lodge. All these months working during daylight and sleeping at night messed up my sleep schedule whenever I returned to Sosnakrev.

Dusan was gone when I returned to the house. Good. Maybe he had to walk off his energy like I did. Or maybe he ran off to tell Casimir that I violated the unspoken rule not to have sex the night before the full moon, so she would get all of our escalating energy.

Agitated, I flared my wings wide. Words didn't attach themselves to all I felt inside. Turned on. Angry. Grieving.

I picked up the blankets, still lying in a heap on the couch, and inhaled Juniper's scent. It was the musky freshness I wanted in my life. I *needed*.

The way she'd responded when my brother watched me take her... Fuck. I'd never done something like that before. It felt different than the moon ritual. There, everything was feral, primal creatures grabbing blindly for each other. I rarely noticed or cared who was watching. But this time, with Juniper, it was...

I ran my hand over my cool face. I was breathing too fast. Sucking a salt bead, I stood in the middle of the room, getting hard thinking about what just happened. Juniper would have words for it. She paid such close attention.

I'd tried to protect her by not explaining everything about my family. I didn't want to leave her to help rule Sosnakrev with Dusan. Vampires understood me and I understood them, but I felt completely stifled here.

I growled. It didn't matter what I did. Juniper and I would never be together. Others could have perfect mates that worked, but I had to fall for a faun.

My presence in Nyx threw a shadow on her credibility among the more peaceful beings. My ties to Sosnakrev already made me leave her regularly so no one got hurt. My responsibilities here meant there would always be some reason I couldn't support her as fully as I wanted to.

Maybe the best thing to do was to follow her advice. Return to Sosnakrev. Help Dusan. Live on the memory of the most perfect, lovable female I'd ever known.

I was shaking. Salt beads wouldn't help me for long.

*Ten deep breaths.*

I got through two before I shouted and knocked over a cold candelabra.

Just more proof that she deserved someone better than me.

Tomorrow would be torture. She'd be tied on the platform while everyone else was below. Just watching. Every muscle in my body would want to climb up to her. That was allowed—the problem was that we dedicated her to the moon. I wasn't allowed to untie her. The only bond strong enough to unleash her would be if I claimed her as my perfect mate.

Binding her to me instead.

I couldn't risk it. As much as I wanted Juniper—*loved* Juniper with so much of my soul that I doubted any sliver existed that she hadn't touched—I couldn't admit the truth. If I didn't claim her, she would be free to become the leader of the Assembly and do all the incredible things she was born to do. Only a monster would hold her back.

BY THE TIME COOKS BROUGHT OUT THE PRE-RITUAL FEAST IN the late afternoon, my mood hadn't lifted. If anything, it had gotten worse.

Despite the black curtains smothering the sunlight, I'd barely slept because my thoughts kept circling like bats around the one thought I dreaded most. Losing Juniper.

My waking hours last night were little better. When I passed a former friend on the street, I realized he'd never met Juniper. When I watched one of the preparators pick up an order of knives from the shop inside a metal-reinforced tree, I remembered bruising and scratches I'd left on Juniper's body when it got too close to moon days. When I passed a small monument to Lord Balaur, the half-demi-god founder of

Sosnakrev, I pictured Juniper's cute expression of rapt concentration whenever she learned something new.

Today made me snappy, on edge. Completely unlike my normal self, even this time of the month. I couldn't tolerate this tension. Tonight, I'd get an outlet, but it would feel hollow without Juniper to share it with me.

For most beings (I learned in Nyx), "feast" usually meant people sitting around a full table, eating and talking. Vampires were too volatile the day of the moon to act polite. Instead, a huge amount of food filled heavy wooden tables starting a couple hours before sundown. Puddings and steaks, sweetmeats and hunks of cheese piled high. We were encouraged to eat as much as possible until sunset. Even those not participating that month got to eat. A sad sort of consolation, when all everyone wanted to do was enter the sacred clearing and release that pent-up feral energy. The space between sunset and moonrise would strengthen us, and then, the ritual.

Someone bumped into me as I tore off a hunk of cured meat. I snarled in response. The female snarled back.

I stuffed the food in my mouth, letting its salty juices calm me. With a calmer outlook, I scanned the table. What could Juniper eat? I snatched a cloth from the edge of the table and started filling it with cheese and bread.

Juniper hadn't arrived at the feast yet, but it wasn't as if it had an official start. No one rang a bell or knocked on doors. So much of this day came down to ancestral memory. Maybe Juniper didn't even know it was happening.

Guilt twisted my gut. Just as I turned to hurry down the trail to the stag lodge, Juniper emerged onto the path, wearing a thick coat. I hadn't even realized it was cold. Now that I paid attention, my breath frosted the air in front of my nose.

"Here," I said, handing her the parcel of food.

Her eyes widened in surprise. The feast looked huge in her arms.

I almost laughed at myself. I was such a brute. All my sensibilities were abandoning me. Did I normally say hello first? Did I actually live with this divine fucking creature?

"What's this?" she asked.

"The feast. The food we put out before the ritual. So we have energy."

Her little mouth formed an O. "I heard about that last night. Should we go sit down?" she asked tentatively.

"It's not like that. Just take it and go—that's how it works."

As she nodded, her brown eyes looked sunken. She hadn't slept either. I fisted my hand to keep from touching the skin there with my fingertips.

A sharp pain speared my chest. I knew but hadn't really known my decision until right then.

This was it for us. I would only return to Nyx to gather my things, and then I'd return to Sosnakrev. For all its faults, I did love this place where I grew up. I wanted Dusan to succeed. I was a vampire to my very core, despite my perfect mate being a faun.

"Did you make any of this?" she asked, stuffing some cheese into her mouth.

Watching the food disappear between her lips had my dick hardening. "No. I would have added sauce."

She chewed thoughtfully, then followed the cheese with a

bit of bread. "Because you're a better cook," she finally declared.

I couldn't stop the half-smile from sneaking onto my face. "Of course I am."

"I had to be sure," she teased.

My heart burned painfully. "They take away the feast at sunset, so get all you need."

"I won't need too much, will I?" Her eyes were understanding but sad. She probably realized before I did that our relationship wouldn't survive past today.

The urge to take her, kiss her, fuck her senseless had me dizzy. *Assembly*, I tried. *Goals. Prejudice. Responsible choices.* The words all sounded stupid in my head. The moon stirred my insides to soup.

"I'd... stay out of the village today," I gritted out. Dusan stayed out of my way when I woke up a couple hours ago, but I overheard him talking to someone about the violent incidents that happened the night before—all young vampires newly touched by the moon's vitality, except for Dusan himself, of course, but no one was seriously injured there.

"What?" Juniper protested. "I wanted to see it!"

"Full moon day. No one is safe. We're used to it. You..."

She shifted her weight, obviously annoyed. "I'm here to research."

"I thought you were here to know me better." That sounded mean. I shouldn't be talking to her today.

"That is research! Learning more about vampires means learning more about you."

"What you learn today will tell you all you need to know about me."

She pressed her lips together. I wanted to bite them. My fangs extended slightly in my closed mouth. Where were my salt pills?

"Please," I urged. "Stay safe."

"I'm not afraid of vampires," she said, leveling a look at me that almost made me get on my knees.

"I know." The words came out breathy. Most were afraid of vampires, with good reason. Our primal selves were terrifying, like the deathless were terrifying, like the wind and the waves were terrifying. One of my favorite things about being a vampire, in its right place, was also a curse and a stigma. "Don't talk to anyone."

"Luca."

"You saw Dusan last night."

We paused. I meant his fight in the street, but her liquid eyes and heightened pulse told me she remembered when Dusan had stared at our ferocious sex without looking away. Juniper liked to be watched. Why was I learning this about her at the same moment I couldn't enjoy it?

Would she like watching me?

I flexed my jaw. "It isn't safe. Eat food and I'll see you at the ritual."

Juniper's forehead creased. "Luca."

I took a long breath to even my emotions. "You'll have a good view up there. You'll learn a lot." I tried for a smile and failed.

"Too bad I can't bring my pad and pen," she said, but the joke fell flat.

"Just stay safe." If anyone harmed her, I'd rip their throat out, Dusan and Casimir be damned.

"I'll try." She shifted the cloth full of food to one arm, so she could reach out a free hand. With an impossibly gentle touch, she stroked my arm from elbow to wrist. She might as well have said, "I love you."

I couldn't swallow past the rock in my throat to say goodbye, so, brute as I was, I simply turned and left.

Cheese turned in my stomach. Looking up, above the line of vampire women, I watched the moon rise above the pines. A coppery scent tanged the air. Blood.

A familiar thrill of discovery made me shiver. Yes, this was dangerous, but I'd finally know all about the fabled moon ritual that vampires had been so tight-lipped about for centuries.

I only wished Luca could be here with me. Males entered on the other side of the clearing. Hopefully, I'd see him as soon as I went in.

The line moved forward steadily toward a pointed black pagoda-shaped pavilion about eight people in front of me. Each female paused there, and then moved beyond. The clearing had to be just past that checkpoint.

Compared to the males, females didn't demonstrate as much rage. Their muscles still bunched and eyes darkened, their leathery wings contracted and shook out, but they didn't seem as impulsive. Anticipation still pulsed through the group. Each step forward was followed by an impatient shuffle toward the pavilion.

I was shorter and thicker than any pale-skinned vampire here. No one had ears like mine, legs like mine. My hips were substantially wider than theirs. I was a vegetarian. It took a lot to make me self-conscious, but this situation was ridiculous. I giggled. Maybe it was just my nerves.

The hours between Luca bringing me food and everyone moving either indoors or into lines felt like forever. I saw Dusan once. I didn't make eye contact. Awkwardness filled my limbs when I saw him. Besides, he was probably in no mood to see me, since he'd lost the right to go into the ritual himself only the day before. He acted like he didn't see me, but in that way that animals acted ignorant when they clearly listened to every move. A slight distraction in the eyes, a tilt of the head. That head tilt was such a Luca movement that I wondered how I didn't see the family resemblance before. Dusan strode past me and others showed him deference—not as much as Casimir got, but still, respect. I had just caught him on a bad day, and then in a compromising position. No surprise that he didn't feel sure about my presence here.

"Take this," someone said to the woman under the pagoda. "Bare yourself to the moon."

I drew air in slowly through my teeth. Deep breathing always calmed Luca down. Right now, I felt like the primal moon energy was playing with me too.

I was next. Once the vampire in front of me took off her clothes—she was gorgeous, like they all were—I stepped up.

An old vampire woman stared at me from where she sat in

near total darkness. Luca's eyesight could pierce darkness like this, but mine couldn't. I squinted. She wore a white dress to the neck, and her black hair had been curled and piled in an elaborate style on her head.

"You're a faun."

"Yes. Lord Casimir said I was allowed to participate."

A young assistant standing near her whispered in the older one's ear.

"Ah. Moon sacrifice." The old woman handed me one of the parcels Viviana had made the night before. "Take this."

I didn't tell her about getting one the day before and dutifully swallowed it dry.

"Bare yourself to the moon."

My throat constricted. If everyone else did it, being naked wasn't weird, right? I shuffled off my clothes, shivering in the cold air. My nipples immediately went hard. The young assistant spirited away the pile of clothes into a series of marked baskets at the far end of the pagoda. At least I could find my clothes again when this was done.

I walked on, as I'd seen others do. Past the shelter of the roof, I gasped. A large round hollow carved into a swath of the landscape, totally bare of trees, which stood like guards all around it. To my left, curving around, there were three high platforms, seven or eight buckets like I'd seen last night dug into the ground, and ten big drums each manned by a drummer. All that took up about half the circumference of the hollow. Across from the pagoda was another similar structure. Naked male figures emerged from that end of the forest to join the female figures already on the green. The pale vampires darted here and there, terrifyingly fast. A snarl rose from the open space below, but no one spoke. Eerily quiet, like the sucking silence before an eruption.

"You're the moon sacrifice?"

I blinked rapidly, focusing on the person who'd spoken close to my ear. A young, clothed vampire—I honestly couldn't tell the gender—offered their hand politely. Maybe they weren't affected by the moon like most other vampires were. I sensed none of the latent violence from them that I sensed from everyone else, even the old woman under the pavilion.

"Yes, I am."

"This way."

I followed them along the lip of the hollow to the nearest platform. With the full moon shining above, it wasn't hard to see the features of the vampires below well enough to identify them. Luca wasn't here yet.

My guide ushered me up a wooden ladder to the top of the bare platform. There was no railing on the small square, just a contraption that looked like a gallows on the side overlooking the clearing. My heart beat faster. We weren't as high as the trees, but I still felt much too far from the ground.

"Arms up."

I unclasped my wringing hands and did what the vampire told me. Facing the hollow, under the moon, I raised my hands. The vampire—who was stronger than they looked—snatched my wrists and bound them with the rope hanging from the frame. Heat shot between my legs. Having my wrists tied above my head reminded me of Luca's wildest nights. I loved this position.

Too bad.

"The painters will be here soon," said my guide. Acolyte—

is that what Luca had called people like this? Every action had been so professional, impersonal even. They chanted a short phrase in another language and descended the ladder.

I strained to remember the words they had spoken, but I could already tell I'd forget by the end of the night. My only choice was to observe and embrace what was happening. No chance I'd catch every detail, though I itched to document everything.

The hollow slowly filled with vampires. None of them touched each other, but the atmosphere trembled with ferocious anticipation.

Glancing to my left, I saw no other moon sacrifices. There must sometimes be more than one. Not tonight, though. Tonight, I was alone.

My attention returned to the people below. *Luca, Luca, Luca...*

There he was! Did he see me dangling here, totally bare, totally vulnerable? He'd want to protect me. Hopefully, he'd keep one eye on me to make sure I was okay. But I wouldn't count on it. Tonight, he wouldn't be himself.

My throat worked with nerves.

The hollow went quiet. Only the soft creaking of ladder rungs broke the silence. It was as if the moon herself buzzed and hissed like a low fire.

I twisted my head to see a young female vampire hauling a small bucket and brush to the landing. She stopped just behind me, not saying a word. That coppery scent I noticed earlier rose forcefully from the bucket in her hands.

Blood.

*Boom!*

All ten drums sounded at once. I watched in awe as the drummers beat in unison again, raising thick drumsticks high above their heads. No one else moved.

*Boom boom boom! Boom boom boom!*

The deep drumbeats picked up their tempo. Then half started playing a different rhythm, creating an irresistible syncopation. I found myself bobbing my head. The rhythms crisscrossed, expertly intricate, but following our pulse at the same time. The music grew desperate. All the intricacies started melding together again into fewer rhythms until finally only a single unified beat was left. The drummers raised their sticks high and sounded one final time. The beat echoed low and pulsed through my body as the noise faded.

I held my breath.

The drummers called out the foreign words. A dedication to the moon?

Like a battle cry, everyone in the hollow responded.

Back and forth, louder and louder, but practiced and precise. The energy below reached an intensity that frightened me. What were rules to vampires truly set loose? How could I defend myself if things went wrong?

A final shouted word echoed across the hollow, and I held my breath...

Movement erupted. It looked like a battle. In seconds, it was difficult to make out anyone's features because they were obscured by everyone else's. I lost Luca in the crowd.

Something cold splashed on me.

"Ah! What—?" I looked down and a large bloodstain dripped down my sides. The breeze blew across the rest of the blood on my lower back.

The young vampire stepped in front of me, paintbrush in hand. There was barely enough space for another person to stand without falling off the edge, but she seemed totally unafraid. Well, she had wings and I didn't. Notoriously, fauns tended to break their ankles when they fell.

She dipped the paintbrush into the small bucket and drew it out dripping with blood. She painted my neck and shoulders, my breasts, my belly, and hips. Circular streaks covered my entire midsection.

For the first time, I wondered how long the ritual would go on. All night, people had told me, but was it really? It was okay to be painted in blood to learn more about another culture's customs, but to stay up here, all feeling draining from my hands while foreign blood grew sticky on my belly for hours in the chill? That didn't sound fun.

As the painter edged away, I offered a small, close-lipped smile, like a thank you. I didn't know what else to do. Would she come back?

The drummers started up again, beating a new rhythm as the ritual continued. I still couldn't find Luca. He was down there somewhere, and... I missed him. It wasn't just his body, that shocking pleasure like I felt last night. It was *him*.

So many little things pointed to the truth that I wasn't his perfect mate—the way he acted so distant here, didn't want me to know about his family, wouldn't say he loved me. Letting him go was the right thing for both of us, but I would miss him horribly. No one believed in me like he did. I loved that we were so different, but we'd made a home anyway. I'd miss his wings and the way he was so careful not to bite or hurt me. The way he made me dinner. The playful look he sometimes got. The way he'd leave his shirt off when he cleaned. The way he'd ask me to dance and then systematically curse the names of everyone who messed up my plans at work.

I sniffed. It wasn't the same between us now. We were awkward.

A hysterical laugh bubbled up. Awkward was an understatement. I was tied up naked like a slaughtered pig above half his village as they had a wild orgy.

Something touched me. My skin flinched away from it. It was a person. It was a... tongue.

Fingers wrapped around my hips as the person settled on their knees to lick my lower back. I twisted to see who it was.

A male with long black hair, maybe a little older than Luca. Behind him, two more vampires topped the ladder. Well, one climbed the ladder and the other half-flew, half-jumped. Faster than I could see, one of them rushed in front of me. I sucked in a breath, heart hammering. Could Luca see me? Was this normal?

Of course it was. I was freaking out because I was a faun told to hide from danger, not run into vampire orgies. By stepping into this clearing under the full moon, I gave my consent to this experience.

I tried to relax. The vampire in front of me was another male, who ran his hands the length of my blood-soaked torso before pressing our bodies together in a kiss. He was muscular and already rock-hard. It wasn't too difficult to kiss him back.

*Still want it to be Luca instead.* Where was he? Why hadn't he been the first up that ladder?

The third vampire pivoted me toward him so he could lick my neck, and lower. He sucked the tip of one breast into his mouth and swirled the nipple on his tongue. His gentle, lover-like movements quickly became more intense.

All three of them snatched and grabbed and took, never reaching between my legs, as promised, but their contact with me clearly aroused them enough that they'd have to abandon me soon to fuck somebody else.

As it was, these three showed more restraint than most of the others moving the ground. Maybe they liked to start slow. A growl ripped from one of their throats, then another. Were they going to fight each other on this little platform? My chest rose and fell faster. I'd seen the violence of a quick brawl before. These three were taller, vibrating with explosive moon energy. They wouldn't even notice me until the fight was over.

"There's enough for everyone," I panted, adjusting my position.

Moon sacrifices were supposed to be safe, but right now, with three vampires vying to touch me and Luca nowhere in sight, I didn't feel safe at all.

# 16

## LUCA

I entered the moonlit clearing behind Casimir. Since Dusan wasn't here, I was basically second-in-command.

Straining to hold onto sanity a beat longer, I watched the leader's winged back as he stalked confidently down into the hollow. Drummers stood at the ready, the scent of blood floated through the chilly air, and my body and mind fell into familiar patterns of moon madness. I usually looked forward to this release, this connection with my clan. Part of me hated that I needed this so desperately and the rest of me relished the sheer vampirism of it. Other races might not understand, but no vampire judged another for this ritual.

I did my best to wrench my mind away from the moon's grip, to think straight, remind myself of what I needed to do. I had to act like Juniper wasn't here.

Impossible.

But necessary, so she wasn't tethered to someone who would hold her back. Bruise her. Cast doubt on her suitability to lead.

I knew that feeling too well, and didn't want her to suffer it as well.

More nude vampires—some whose lips already dripped red —congregated around us. Lustful looks were cast my way. Before, this part was easy, natural. At least, I knew that once the drummers started, I could release myself in a savage abandonment with the rest of my clan.

Now, the knowledge that Juniper was here gnawed at my insides, leaving them a bloody mess. All I wanted was for her to be with me.

*Let her go. Let her go. Take your secret to the grave.*

My focus pulled up to the platforms, where I knew she'd be. I couldn't help it. Strung up near the edge of the wooden landing, she hung, wrists bound, gloriously naked. The moon caught her bronze curls. Because her hooves were so small compared to her hips, it looked like she was on tiptoe.

My dick immediately grew thick and hard. Painful.

If I hadn't known she was my perfect mate before, I would have learned right then. Her body, her soul, *everything* called to me with a strength I'd never felt before. It was as if a line hooked through my torso onto my spine and physically yanked my body toward hers.

Coherent thoughts disappeared.

She was all.

*Boom!*

The drums started. I, along with everyone else, vibrated with eagerness and intensity. My mouth watered. My balls ached.

High up on the platform, an acolyte splashed blood on Juniper's back. She flinched at the contact. I bared my teeth.

The painter swirled moon circles on her back and chest in red. Delicious red I could lick off her body.

I was panting, couldn't remember why I shouldn't join her there.

*Moon sacrifice. Can't take her down. Only if I claim her as my perfect mate. Then she'd be trapped with me.*

I closed my eyes, but that only heightened my other senses—the soil gritting under my bare feet, the smell of pine trees, the undefinable moon energy that pulsed through all of us...

The drums stopped. Drummers called. We responded as one. I beat my chest. Even Casimir, our leader, became just another body in the clearing with the rest of us, reveling in the primal togetherness like we all were.

A breath, and then... chaos. Everyone rushed at each other, grasping and pulling so forcefully I heard grunts and screams as clusters of vampires went down. Someone grabbed my arm, but I didn't move. I couldn't. My eyes locked on Juniper and her blood-stained, freckled skin.

Three vampires surrounded her, touching her, licking off the blood, their stiff cocks evident. My heart jogged too fast in my chest. Juniper's posture was too rigid. The ritual made us fluid or desperate, not stock-still.

But here I was. I wasn't right. This wasn't right. Moon energy crawled inside me but it couldn't get out. All my self strained toward Juniper on that platform.

Something touched my thigh. It was my own shaking fist.

Reasons evaporated and primal need roared free.

Juniper was mine. No one else's. She was my mate, the one who belonged in my life and soul. I was made for her. Arguments beat uselessly against that knowledge, but I swiped at them with clawed certainty.

Unfurling my wings, I sped toward her. My little-used wings ached like sex at the rigorous movement and it only drove me crazier.

Juniper spotted me coming. Her eyes rounded with hope and fear.

Unleashing a savage cry, I yanked the first vampire off her by his neck, sending him tumbling off the edge of the landing.

Juniper gasped, but I wasn't finished.

I tossed the other two off next, who were too drunk on sex and moon madness to register my attack until it was too late.

With Juniper alone, one thought lit up my whole being. *My mate.* She had to get off this fucking platform. She didn't belong to the moon anymore. She belonged to me. With me. And I belonged to her, everything else be damned.

Snarling with need, I untied her hands, clutched her in my arms, and jumped off the side.

# 17

# JUNIPER

I screamed as the platform dropped away to open air.

Night whipped around us. Luca held me tightly as we fell. My stomach plummeted. What was he doing? Was he going to end it all here at a vampire orgy?

Unfurling his wings, he caught the air so fast I grunted. Even with that hitch, there wasn't a whisper of him letting me go. He was strong before, but now he was something legendary. His black wings spread wide on either side of us. I'd never seen him fly like this—I knew he could, but this was awe-inspiring. Each beat of his wings throbbed against my eardrums.

And it wasn't only his wings that came alive. Luca's face glowed with life. His entire body did. His expressive eyes burned. Had his neck always been that muscular? Had the place where it met his shoulder always been so enticing?

He pitched upward, panting like he'd run a race. His naked chest pressed against mine so I felt every breath.

Luca wasn't taking me away to keep me safe, or stopping

me from being part of the ritual. When he turned his flaming eyes on me, the look was all possession, need. It said *MINE*. This went beyond a dark night when he found my wrists back home. It was more than lust—it was a whole godsdamned lot of lust, but it was more than that. The look didn't say *mine now*. It said *mine forever. My perfect mate.*

Above was the shining moon and below was a mass of writhing vampires. The wind dried some of the sticky blood covering my torso, gluing me to Luca. I didn't need to be tangled together and stuck to him to feel how rock hard he was. His dick tapped me with every movement. With every pulse of his wings, he groaned, flexing his hips. My legs wrapped around his waist but we couldn't connect.

One arm holding me readjusted so he could grab my ass. For a split second we fell again as he fit himself into my sopping pussy.

I shrieked, unable to stop myself. Luca gave a wild, toothy grin.

"You," he said, flapping those massive wings again. "I claim you, Juniper." Each pulsating beat of the wings meant an echoing one between my legs. He managed to look me in the eye, his glistening black hair backlit by the moon. "Perfect mate."

A tiny part of me wanted to tease him for denying those existed, but most of me wanted to let my head fall back and give in to the thrusting pleasure.

We were wild.

We were wild *together*. In the air above a vampire orgy.

Hopefully it wasn't just the ritual making him say these

things. The insistent roll of his hips churned away any doubts. Luca wouldn't throw around those words.

Flying and fucking and holding me with those metal-strong arms... I stopping thinking at all. Only his body and mine as snarls and cries of ecstasy echoed below. We circled the ritual ground above the trees a little longer before descending.

Drums beat heady rhythms. Acolytes carried their paint-brushes. Vampires were everywhere, licking blood, tangled in knots, baring their teeth, sucking each other.

I couldn't look away. I really was prey among predators. Luca's kind was dangerous and violent and sexual in a way fauns never were.

Maybe the moon madness was on me too, but I liked it.

I wanted Luca to tackle me and pin me down, force himself inside me and leave marks declaring I was his. I'd never get tired of hearing the words or seeing the truth in his eyes. I was his.

As soon as my hooves touched the ground, he shoved me, bending me backward over something moving. I was on someone else's back, wings flaring on either side of my neck.

"Oh!" I exclaimed.

"Don't move." He parted my legs and plunged even deeper.

I couldn't help but stiffen since my spine was moving with somebody else. Not Luca. What was free and wild and sexy in the air now made me almost self-conscious. The broad back underneath me moved rhythmically, finding pleasure of its own. Almost like the person wasn't surprised to have a faun spread over them as her perfect mate drilled into her.

I matched my breathing to Luca's movements. He still felt

good—he always felt good—but I wasn't lost in him like I'd been in the air.

His frenzied expression cleared a fraction, just enough for me to see that he understood what I was thinking.

"I will make you forget everyone and everything," he growled. "You'll surrender."

Something splashed on me. More blood. Salty and thick, it ran down my sides. All my curiosity and research hadn't prepared me for something so feral. With a groan, Luca crouched to lick me, scraping my skin with his teeth. He was usually so careful not to do that. To prevent temptation, he said. Now, his pointed canines pinched my hip. I gasped.

As if I'd summoned them with that noise, two other vampires stalked over. They were beautiful. I couldn't get over how everyone here was beautiful. Dark hair and pale skin and long, tall bodies. They bent to feast on the blood running over my torso.

Luca snarled possessively but then let them run their tongues over me. I opened my mouth—shouldn't I push them off?—but thought better of it. The clan seemed to understand whatever boundary he set. Maybe it was just that I was his mate, no one else's, but since it was the full moon ritual, we all could continue together. I trusted Luca regardless. If he let these vampires touch me, I'd focus on the sensation.

The moon didn't control me the way it obviously controlled the vampires, but the atmosphere still intoxicated me. What if I let go, stopped stiffening, and fully joined the ritual with Luca? What we'd done felt wild enough, but there were a hundred more winged bodies looking for pleasure and release.

What had Noula said? *"I probably wouldn't mind getting railed by an entire vampire clan, if I could survive it."* Luca would make sure I did.

I let my head fall back. The female vampire sucked my breast, the male rubbed against my side, and Luca's head bobbed between my legs. Experimentally, I swept a hand down the newcomers' legs, just seeing what it would be like to encourage this.

My last threads of resistance loosened. Drums pounded and we all matched the rhythm. In the darkness hid this wild secret, this primal part of ourselves. The part that reached for more flesh, more contact, more grinding pressure where I needed it.

Luca was up again, but the ritual, to me, had become a dance or a fight. I didn't pull him back down. There was a rhythm to everything—our panting breaths, my throbbing sex... We had all night.

Drunk with lust, I watched Luca kiss the male next to me, holding him fiercely by the back of the neck. I thought it might bother me to see him like this, touching people other than me, but I was here too, and I was touching him, touching them, feeling the hard length of them in each hand, kissing someone else.

*My gods.* I didn't know myself. I was moon madness. Luca stayed by me, directing people's mouths to pleasure me, directing me to pleasure others, all in a way that felt like some kind of choreographed struggle. Grasping hands held hard, mouths bit lightly enough not to pierce the skin, movements alternated between sensually slow and vampire fast.

Luca wasn't thinking straight—I knew that. Neither was I.

But I couldn't help feeling that he wanted me to experience it all, everything. From being crushed between two thrusting bodies, to lying in a tangle, to a more violent push and pull as the vampires took what they wanted.

Despite the cold, sweat covered my body. I burned from the inside. Stunning people licked it off in long, languorous strokes. Releasing a sigh when someone moved off to another partner, I found Luca in the melee. He was riding Viviana and instantly met my eye. I gave him a sloppy, open-mouthed smile.

A large figure stalked forward, past Luca, to me. He was craggy, muscular, with huge wings.

Luca watched as Casimir sized me up. I stood my ground, pulse ricocheting off my ribs. In the throes of the madness, would he forget he'd allowed me here? Would he be angry that Luca claimed me as his mate?

"Luca!" he ordered. "Hold her up."

Those were more coherent words than I'd heard all night. No wonder Casimir led the clan. Everyone else just hissed out *shit* or *fuck, there!*

Luca obeyed, positioning himself behind me and hoisting me up. It was as if I were weightless. His fingers dug into my inner thighs as he spread me for his leader.

I dripped in anticipation, as eager for sex as any vampire here.

Casimir crashed into me. Luca took one step backward, anchoring himself.

Held in my mate's stable arms, I winced at the pressure as Casimir rammed his dick into me. He reached around and gripped not me, but Luca, and brought us both against him again and again. The grunts of the two males on either side of me hurtled me to the edge. Casimir pressed in deep, squeezing me against Luca's chest, and I lost control. My thighs trembled and a high-pitched yell gusted from my lips.

Suspended between them, I let my head loll back on Luca's shoulder. He kissed me as Casimir tasted the sweat from my chest.

The more covered in sweat I became, the more other vampires were drawn to me. They ran cold. Less sweat. But Luca had taught me how delicious it could be.

When I opened my eyes, I stood on the ground again. Casimir was gone. Someone had pulled Luca away, and a newcomer kissed my lower stomach. My eyes rolled back when they reached the apex of my thighs.

*All the gods and Hades…*

A couple times, Luca blinked like he was waking up and caught my eye. I would have laughed at the compromising positions we both were in when that happened. I'd give him a little nod—*yes, I like this; no, what you're doing to that other vampire doesn't bother me*—and we'd fall back under the spell of the moon.

The drums grew more frantic as the night went on. The blue light grew brighter over all of us. The moon was almost at its peak.

Two of the male vampires crowding me broke out in a fight, almost dropping me. I caught myself in time. Their scuffle become a desperate grasp at limbs, a fight to suck the other dry.

I moaned, past the point of ordinary arousal. I was thirsty and sex-drunk and one with Luca in a way I never imagined possible, even when I pictured this ritual. Hands gripped my wrists and spun me around. Luca again. He crushed his lips to mine and found my sex with his fingers, working furiously at the spot only he knew how to find so fast.

Already primed, my need spiked. "Yes... yes!" I cried to every third drumbeat.

His tongue swept into my open mouth before he bit down hard on my lip.

"Yes... yes!"

And then, his teeth found a vein in my neck and, without hesitation, he bit there too.

# 18

## LUCA

Juniper's blood tasted like caramel.

Once, she cut herself and offered to let me taste it, but I declined. I knew I wouldn't be able to stop, that I'd be so aroused and so maddened by the taste that I'd keep sucking and sucking and sucking...

I was right.

She was everything I suspected. All those nights when I fought off the urge to do just this clattered around like idiocy in my head. Why hadn't I enjoyed all of her? Not only her hot, slick sex, but her salty, delicious blood too? It was too much.

My hand moved to her full hip. There was so much more of her there than the lean hips of the vampires. Why didn't everyone want a faun? And why was I lucky enough to have Juniper beat in my chest and in my mouth as my perfect mate?

My fangs sank deeper into her neck. Juniper whimpered, egging me on. I pulled more of her blood into my mouth. A growl escaped my lips at just how fucking good she tasted.

Nothing I'd ever concocted in the kitchen came close to the delicacy of sucking her.

Her hand on my stone-stiff cock released its pressure. She was wilting in my arms. I held her closer, running my tongue along her pierced skin to lap up the bleeding. A drip dribbled from my mouth.

Coming up for air, I gasped, rocking with moon energy, taking new handfuls of Juniper. Other hands and bodies collided with us, but they didn't matter. Not after tasting Juniper's blood.

I looked down.

Her eyes were closed, face almost as pale as mine. Her small mouth was open, but not in that inviting way. Two streaks of red ran down her neck where I'd feasted on her. Her throat looked bruised around the points where my canines had sunk into her.

I jostled her, a kernel of dread growing in my chest.

The moon, full and directly above us, shone on her unmoving face.

"Juniper." Panic found a place inside me. I licked my lips.

It was the ritual and I couldn't think straight. I only had arousal and anger and panic and ferocious longing for this adorable female. The one who was mine.

"Juniper!"

Again, nothing.

Still holding her up, I grabbed one of the acolytes by the arm as he passed. "Water," I snarled. "Now." Pushing him away, I turned back to Juniper.

All around rose the wails and slaps and moans of wild ecstasy, but my ecstasy was withering behind my ribs.

Even the moon wasn't stronger than my love for Juniper. She looked so small in my arms, stained and naked. She was perfect, and I had bitten her.

I swore I never would, but...

*You knew this would happen. You knew she'd get hurt.*

As if in answer, someone nearby cried out.

I didn't suspect that I'd be the one to hurt her.

"Juniper," I tried again, moving wet hair away from her forehead.

Her eyes moved behind her lids.

I exhaled sharply. Her skin felt warm. I repositioned her so we were even closer, tangled together chest to chest. "Water! Where is it?" I roared.

The young vampire reappeared with a cup. It was a little bloody on the edges, but I didn't care. I splashed a little on Juniper's face and then poured a sip into her mouth. She swallowed.

*Good girl.*

I did it again, then set down the cup to wrap my fingers around her throat, closing up the wound without closing off her air supply.

"Juniper."

She blinked and groaned, hazily meeting my eyes.

I drew her into a tight hug. "I... didn't mean to..."

"I'm okay," she breathed in my ear.

"I'm sorry. You were... so delicious." I shouldn't have said it, but I felt delirious. The moon was full and I was nothing but feral, honest energy. Helping Juniper felt like waking up from a dream that was dragging me down again. A strange surge of pride filled me that our bond was strong enough to take me out of the moon's madness.

I felt her smile against my neck. "Delicious?"

"So delicious," I moaned.

"I'm okay," she repeated.

Not even angry. She wasn't even angry. "I love you," I burst out.

She twined her arms around me, teasing the wings. I shivered at the touch. "I love you too," she answered. My kisses smothered her next words. "Luca. Perfect mate."

I was already parting her plump thighs again when she said, "Oh! Is that water?" She reached over my arms to pick up the cup. I watched her throat move as she gulped the drink down. "The ritual is tiring work," she said, eyes twinkling.

I smirked. "I've decided I get you the rest of the night to myself. Unless you want to bring someone in. I'm not leaving."

A line furrowed between her eyebrows. "The ritual... You want it to be just us? Does that make sense?"

"You. I only want you. I want to taste you and fuck you and bring you so much pleasure you'll never recover. I'm addicted to you, Juniper. Even more than the moon. Even more than my entire clan." I looked up at her shining brightly above the trees. "My bond with you is stronger. So, yes. If it will bring you more pleasure, bring in anyone you want. But you're mine." I fisted my cock between us and pushed it into her.

Her eyes glazed. "Our ritual."

"Our ritual," I echoed, grinding close in those circles she craved.

Beautiful bodies surrounded us, blood-soaked and writhing with shared lust, but we stayed at the center, sure as a rock in the ocean. Declaring her my perfect mate meant more than words. It connected me to her closer than I thought possible. She lived inside me as surely as I pulsed inside her. I'd protect and pleasure her till my dying day.

Fuck anyone who said fauns and vampires couldn't be together. Juniper and I would live in our little house. One day, she'd be the head of the Assembly and I'd be so godsdamned proud of her. Nyx was lucky to have her. Hell, the world was lucky to have her in it.

And I got to hold her in my arms and feel her suck along my length. Unbelievable.

A small horde of other vampires surrounded us—Juniper allowed them in—all contracting wings and rolling bodies. Juniper was the shortest of them all. Her soft ears reached my chest as we stood in the center, pressed together, straining again for release. She looked up at me. I looked down at her. Her liquid brown eyes went knowing. It was a mix of that look she got when she was researching, the way her face lit up and curiosity burned across her features, and the eyes she made when she wanted me to take her to bed.

Tenderness pierced through the violent haze of lust that gripped us all. Even with so many others pressing in, Juniper and I were alone in that moment, surfacing just long enough to share a look that said, *How lucky am I to love you?*

I slowed my pace, gave her a kiss. Her lips tasted like salt. Leaning my forehead against hers, I felt the first breeze that signaled the coming of dawn, and it started to snow.

# 19

# JUNIPER

"This is the one good thing about the stag lodge," Luca explained, soaking the sponge in bathwater.

I swished my foot near his hip. The free-standing bronze tub was big enough for both of us to sit across from each other comfortably. This was my favorite room. The dark walls were carved with astrological symbols and fang-like points echoing the architecture.

"I think there are other good things," I said.

Luca mirrored my smile. "Here." He leaned forward and gently drew the sponge over my collarbone and shoulder.

I winced.

His eyes shone perfectly clear as he searched mine. The madness that had gripped him during the full moon was gone, and in its place was sweet, gentle Luca. "Plenty of tea, water, sleep, and food for the next two days," he said softly.

I smoothed a streak of dirt from his cheek with my thumb. "Whatever you say. You're the expert."

He gave me a light kiss.

Everything hurt, but light still filled up my being. Luca loved me, claimed me publicly as his perfect mate. Finally.

"Why did you wait so long?" I asked.

His deep-set eyes softened. I didn't need to explain what I meant. "I've known for a long time. You're everything to me, Jun. But I see the way people treat you when they know you're with me. Somewhere, I'm sure, I knew my responsibilities would call me back here. There were parts of my life I didn't think you could accept." His mouth quirked into a quiet smirk.

"But then Casimir railed me."

Luca gasped and splashed me.

"While you held me up," I laughed, shielding my face. It was all so absurd. He was right. This shouldn't make sense.

But we did.

"Juniper!" He was laughing too. With a sigh, he said, "Seeing you with the rest of the clan..."

I caressed his cheek. "I'm not promising that I'll do this every month."

"I'd never want that. You have important business. And you can't have bruises all the time."

That was true. Simply getting into this tub had been a symphony of grunts and groans, but the warm water helped, just as Luca had promised.

Bruising and scratches covered Luca's chest and arms too, but satisfaction made the whole wild experience worth it. None of the angry edginess he demonstrated before remained in his eyes.

"What about around my birthday?" he teased.

I rolled my eyes at him. "And if I'm the leader of the Assembly?"

"You'll need to release some stress." A dimple appeared in his half-smile.

But the topic of home sobered us both. For a few moments, we sat in silence.

"Let me do your hair," Luca finally said.

I swiveled around and laid my head in his lap with my face peeking out of the water. He scooped some soap into his palm and massaged my scalp. I closed my eyes, leaning into the delicious sensation.

His fingertips grazed the sensitive spot on my neck. "I shouldn't have bitten you," he whispered.

"I'm okay," I whispered back. The reality of that hadn't fully hit me. Luca could have accidentally killed me. But he didn't. He never would, even when the moon was high. Knowing that was its own kind of liberation. "It felt kind of good."

"Really?"

"Not half as bad as people say."

I felt rather than saw him smile.

"So," I began, unsure. "This is your home—"

"Nyx is my home. With you."

I opened my eyes. Luca's slow hands made lazy circles through my hair as he gazed down at me. "This is your home too. I know I just met Casimir and Dusan on this trip but..."

"They're assholes?"

I bit my lip to keep from smiling. "At first glance." I sat up to face him, water pouring loudly from my hair. "I think Sosnakrev needs you. What do you think?"

He ran a thumb back and forth on my thigh while he

considered. "I think you're right." His expression went impish, a twinkle in his eye. "You're a very wise faun, Juniper."

I gave him a kiss. Our lust was spent, but I still couldn't get enough of his nearness.

"I won't move here permanently," he went on, "not without you. And I'd never ask that."

I nodded.

"But maybe I could split my time."

"I think that's a wonderful idea."

"I could cook for the feast, so you have some better options when you visit."

I grinned. He leaned back against the lip of the tub, his wings poking out above his head and arching over the side. A crooked smile made him irresistible. I kissed him again. As I leaned in, he hooked me in place with one strong arm and pressed his lips to my forehead.

"You're stuck with me now," he said. "Perfect mates are for life."

I squirmed with delight. "That's all I wanted."

Luca released me enough to peer deep into his eyes. Water dripped from his black hair down his temples. The arm still holding me in place felt wonderfully cool. "Even though it might be harder for the Assembly to respect you?"

"Yes. I'll show them so many reasons to respect my ideas that they won't help being on my side."

Luca beamed wide enough to show his pointed canines. "I know you will, you force of nature."

"I'm thinking I'll start with a kind of vampire cultural center if I can get one approved in Nyx. It'll be a place where vampires feel safe and others can come and learn about what vampire communities are like."

He pulled away, releasing me from his hold. I leaned against the opposite end of the tub, gauging his reaction. "Nothing about the moon ritual, remember?"

I laid one hand on the skin above my heart. "I remember. That's ours."

My stomach did a funny flip when Luca smirked. "Exactly."

# 20

# EPILOGUE: JUNIPER

King Hades took his seat at the head of the Assembly. His flinty eyes passed over each of us in turn—mostly gods and demi-gods—where we sat around the big round table. I sat three chairs away from him on a cushion, so I could see eye to eye. Noula told me nobody would notice.

Hades folded his fingers together deliberately before setting them on the tabletop. "Give me updates on Nyx. Make it quick," he said, cocking a brow.

"Crime still persists, my lord," said the demi-goddess to his right. "But this year there have been more burglaries than murders. Smaller-scale crime."

Hades pursed his lips. "Is that trend expected to continue?"

"I..." The demi-goddess fumbled. "The crime or the improvement?"

"The improvement."

She floundered under his attention. Why had she spoken up at all? Didn't she work on economical matters?

I cleared my throat. Hades turned his attention to me. The demi-goddess next to him exhaled.

"I think the rate of crime is likely to improve, King Hades," I said, voice steady.

He pinned me with a searching look that said he would tolerate no lies or apathy about his city. No hint of condescension laced that look.

I straightened my spine. "Since last year, we've begun to open more nocturnal establishments for people who don't prefer sunlight. The city is busier at night than it has ever been before, which means—"

Across the table, someone rolled their eyes.

I shot them a glare. "Which means that it's easier to schedule security shifts at all hours while we are catering to more of our population." With a dry throat, I focused again on the Far Realm's king. "Nyx should be safe and inclusive at all hours, not just in the daytime."

I was incredibly proud of the multi-tiered initiative I started a year and a half ago. So far, with only a few hiccups, it seemed to be improving the lives of more people in Nyx.

"Your husband is a vampire, I believe," Hades said coolly.

Heat rushed to my cheeks. He remembered? Luca's name had come up once at an Assembly meeting months ago. "Yes, Lord Hades. Luca of Sosnakrev."

"Hm." Something like a smile softened his lightly bearded lips. "I like what you've done," he stated in Hingat.

My lips parted in shock. Hades spoke my language?

Then, in the common tongue, he added, "Nyx could use more people like you."

"And then he said, 'Nyx could use more people like you.'" I jumped into Luca's lap with glee. He smelled like roasted onions, but I burrowed my face in his chest anyway.

"That's amazing, Jun!" He cradled my head against him.

"I said I'd get Hades to notice the work I was doing!" I said, face smothered.

"No one can stop you."

I backed up. Luca beamed at me. Little wrinkles crinkled from his eyes.

"How was Sosnakrev?" I asked. He'd been gone a week.

"Casimir made Dusan lead his first formal meeting."

"And that went...?"

"Not as bad as you'd think." He tapped my nose. "You might have been proud."

"*You* were proud of him, at least." I pressed my lips into a teasing expression.

He shrugged. "He's my brother. I helped him through it."

"Is Casimir going to give him the reins now?"

"Gods, I hope he'll wait a while." His eyes twinkled. "That reminds me." He hoisted himself to his feet, holding onto me and taking me with him to the kitchen. "He sent me home with this, for you."

Luca set me on my feet. I peered curiously at the cloth-covered item on the counter. I'd been too excited with my news when I came home to notice the enticing smell.

"Casimir handed the ingredients to me and just said, 'She might like it.'"

I raised both eyebrows.

Luca pulled back the cloth. Underneath was cranberry bread. I covered my mouth and stared. That was one of my favorite things.

"He doesn't hate me!" I exclaimed, rummaging in a drawer for a knife.

Luca kissed the top of my head. "No one could hate you."

I barked a laugh, too joyous to be bitter. "At the meeting today—"

"Fuck them, then. Who are they compared to Hades?"

"No one." I grinned as I attacked the cranberry bread. "This was so nice of him."

"That's going too far. I made the bread. But I'm glad he's finally acknowledging that I'm married to you. That you're never going away."

I paused mid-saw. "No, I'm not," I agreed primly.

"Because you're my perfect mate," he purred.

"And you're mine."

"Fauns don't have fated mates."

I brandished the knife. "Not with that attitude. Now be quiet and eat this cranberry bread with me."

Luca laughed. "I'd prefer something... stronger." His black wings fluttered as he caged me against the counter.

His breath feathered against my mouth, and I felt suddenly drunk on him. "I can arrange that." The new moon was approaching, a safe time, so I drew the blade across my fingertip. "You want this?" I asked sweetly.

Luca's pupils expanded, taking over his irises. He took my

hand in both of his and eased my bleeding finger into his mouth. He released a stifled moan. Against my leg, his bulge grew hard and heavy. My lips curved as I watched him suck down my blood with the greatest ecstasy. Just little bits here and there—enough to tease him, arouse him, but never enough to harm me.

I twisted to grab the first slice of cranberry bread.

It almost didn't seem fair. All my dreams were coming true.

# THANK YOU!

Thank you for reading *Full Moons and Vampires*! Please consider leaving a review. Reviews help authors like me get found by more readers.

Now, read on for a sneak peek of another story that will leave you begging for more...

Or, read *Wings and Blindness*—an Eros and Psyche remix that asks what would happen if Psyche were sent to kill Eros to begin with...

This first book in the Deathless Love series welcomes you to the Eight Realms, where danger and desire lurk in every corner, and mythology isn't quite as you remember it.

Join the Foxy newsletter and read this book FREE!

weat dripped into my eyes. *Not now.* I was about to beat my record. And I needed to break my record today.

Gritting my teeth, I hauled myself higher on the mast. From here, the wind shook more violently, dark sails pressed against my body, and I had fewer handholds, not like the easy rigging lower down. It felt like climbing the trees that bordered the swamplands of my childhood. Except, this time, I hovered above cold waves in tight, leather-fronted pants, a leather vest mended in nine colors of thread, and a blue sash tied around my waist where I could stow knives, tools, and provisions. One of the knife hilts dug into my side where it met the hard length of the pole.

"You're slowing down, sweetheart," Zete called from the deck below.

I didn't look down at him, but the gray flutter of wings told me he was seconds away from flying up here. I wanted to yell back, but that would only waste air. *I'm not done yet.*

But it wasn't lack of air that was slowing me down. It wasn't even the sweat in my eyes from the relentless sunshine. It was this extra weight I felt like I was carrying ever since last week when Calix scoffed in my face.

"You know what?" he'd said. "You're a cold bitch, Mari. I'm done."

I didn't beg to get him back, not after he'd said that. I debated prying off his fingernails for speaking that way to me, but his accusation hollowed me out. All I could do was leave. Looking back, I hated myself for not saying more, doing more. It was the doubt, the stupid doubt that was I worth defending at all. Maybe he was right. He never said it, but I knew I made him feel shitty about himself because I never orgasmed in bed. It wasn't that I didn't enjoy it, I just...

I huffed, reaching the top of the mast and eyeing the next obstacle. Of all the parts of the course I'd laid out for myself, this was the most dangerous. A carefully calculated jump from the highest horizonal yard to the next mast down. There was no way to make the leap straight across. I'd have to angle to reach the ratlines and then scurry back up. If I missed the lines and fell, I'd crash to the hard deck below.

Being a demi-goddess wouldn't stop me from breaking bones. Hell, I could splatter on the deck. Unlike a full goddess, I couldn't crawl back to myself piece by piece if the injury were bad enough. I could only adjust my appearance in small ways—a bend in my nose, freckles there, new eye color and shape—but I couldn't cover up an arm bending at the wrong angle. It wasn't a pretty idea.

Plus, Captain Terion would be furious.

From the corner of my eye, I could see my shipmates pausing to watch me. Zete looked small despite his beard and wings next to massive Ajax. They both gave me hell sometimes, but I knew they didn't want me to get hurt.

I had to stop thinking about Calix. His stupid words threw me off. The sea felt choppy enough up here without more distractions.

"You've got it!" Zete cried from below.

"I know!" I snapped back, balancing myself on the tiny waving platform amid the sails, preparing to spring. One jump and then—

I wobbled and the world turned. My arms flailed out, the deck rose up, and the mast tilted away from me. My feet floated in air. Scrabbling madly, I finally touched something, grasped at rigging, and jarred to a stop. The rest of my body yanked on the arm I'd managed to tangle in the ropes, and a cry ripped from my lips. The dead weight felt like five times the size of my body, but then it bounced up, and the world stilled.

I pressed my face into the squares of rope, squeezing my eyes shut. Pain lanced through my arm and shoulder. I didn't want to look at the others just below me. I'd failed, and I really, really hadn't wanted to fail today.

As if the words had knocked me down, they swirled again and again through my thoughts. *A cold bitch.*

I pictured Calix above me, pumping in. It felt like a slightly painful massage. Not bad. Pretty nice, actually. Yes, I wished I felt more, but for whatever reason I almost never felt that lustful attraction toward anyone, even the people I slept with. I tried—I really did—but there was always something missing for me. Too many factors had to be in place for me to get really turned on, and no single person fit them all.

One reason why I'd always be alone.

I swallowed hard and squeezed the ropes in shaking fists. Normally, I wasn't this shaken up by stupid comments. Why did this one need to feel like a knife to the ribs? I had to get myself together. Maybe stab something.

I had a place here on the *Lusca*, shipmates who tolerated me, a bed and meals. Sure, there was danger, especially after what happened with King Basileus a few years ago, but life was always dangerous. With a deep breath, I relaxed and slowly made my way down.

"Well, at least you're not jelly I need to scrape off the deck," said Zete. He rarely did that kind of work anyway.

Ajax offered his huge arm. Even though he was first mate, I didn't take it. "Think you need Klep?" he asked, apparently unbothered by my slight.

I shook my head, easing my weight to the planking. I'd had injuries like this a million times. No needed to call the medic. Still, my joints twinged as I released my hold on the rope. "No. I'm fine."

Zete squinted at me, lines spidering through his brown skin. "Your shoulder looks off. That was a hard fall. I thought you were supposed to be good at that."

"I'll be fine. I'll do it faster next time." I webbed my power along my shoulder, but it remained a little wonky. At least the bruises wouldn't show now.

Ajax cocked his jaw. "You're no good to the captain if you break everything."

"I'm well aware." My stare finally made him back off. I knew I was being snappy, but I couldn't help it. This week had been a shitshow.

"Mari, you're not even dressed! We dock in half an hour."

I whirled to see Terion swaggering across the planking toward me. He must have come from the lower decks. Instead of wearing his usual captain's jacket and fingerless gloves, he looked... rich. No scarf covering his short black hair, though he still wore his boots. He looked clean and impressive, worthy of all the looks he usually got in pirate-friendly ports. One glance at his impeccable, shimmering blue suit brought a memory slamming back.

Dio's party tonight. The two of us had been planning to go for a month.

How Terion managed to snag an invitation was beyond me. It wasn't normal to invite known pirates to parties where wealthy and powerful people let down their guard. Dio's parties were legendary centers for wine and gambling and sex, any pleasure money could buy.

Which was why we were going to rob him.

"How did you do that to your face?" I asked, pointing at my cheek in the spot where Terion's scales were missing on his face. Instead, there was just smooth dark skin—no regal signature left over from his royal father. Normally, he had a swath of blue-green scales over one cheekbone. Did he find someone else with the ability to change appearances? The idea made me squirm a little.

"You think they'd let me in if they knew who I was?" He laughed. "Come on in, Captain Asterion," he mimicked. "Want a tour of the vaults?"

"Please," I said. No one used his full name like that. He was just Terion or the captain, even to worshippers in his suna. "I said *how* not *why*."

"Ah." He held up a finger. "Forget that. You get ready. I dropped off the dress hours ago. What have you been doing?"

"Obstacles," Zete cut in.

"Again?" Terion's expression became stern. "Mari, haven't you done that enough times already?"

"She was trying to beat her time."

"Almost did," I muttered, stopping myself from rubbing at my injured shoulder.

Terion grunted. "Never mind. I like that in a subordinate. Always getting better." His eyes twinkled roguishly at me. It was the look he always got before a mission. Even with so much on the line, he couldn't deny the call of adventure, just like me.

I burned to ask what he'd been doing that kept him away from the upper deck for so long, but I had already a few guesses. Adventure wasn't the only thing that made Terion smirk like that. He'd picked up a woman at our last port who said she wanted a ride to Hyperion. Maybe she was telling the truth, but a lot of people wanted to board our ship after getting one look at Terion. Honestly, I didn't blame them.

Captain Terion was tall, confident, and muscular with buttery skin and dark, intense eyes. His tone could switch from flirtatious to commanding in a second. The allure of being the most famous Nalian pirate didn't hurt either. Royal, too.

Right now, being one of the abandoned princes was hurting him, but most didn't know he was estranged from his father King Basileus. Well, estranged was a kind way of putting it. Endangered was much more accurate.

Hence, the party.

I scanned the horizon. No visible land yet—I would have noticed it from the top of the mast—but time was running out to get ready. Normally, this kind of assignment got my blood racing. I wasn't good at many things, but I was good at sneaking into places unnoticed and relieving people of their property. That was the reason Terion took me on board to begin with.

"Put on the dress, Mari," he said. His gaze took in my short wind-swept hair and dirty bare feet. "Half an hour. I want you looking like a girl I'd have on my arm."

My face hardened. The things he said sometimes... "You wish you were so lucky."

"I want Dio thinking that."

Something twinged inside me. We'd discussed the possibility of me having to distract Dio, but I hoped to the ocean gods I didn't have to. Everybody rubbed me the wrong way today.

Women at the party would fall all over Terion. It was easy to forget his effect on people when we were on the sea, just shipmates. Too bad I couldn't just leave him to it. If I had to play the part of the sexy date for very long, the hypocrisy of it would scratch under my skin and distract me.

On land, I'd actually seen women begging to come aboard. Terion's whispered reputation talked about his expertise in chains and whips and ruthless but effective domination.

Weird things to hear about a friend, but I didn't doubt it. His default mood was optimistically confident. Vain, even, but a good captain to his sailors. For that, I was lucky. Taken in a different direction, that self-assurance could easily manifest in darker, more intense ways. I'd seen hints of it when I got drunk with him after losing a sailor to Basileus' rage or when he stood on deck, soaking wet and grinning after a bad storm.

One room was off limits to everybody but him—a locked room below deck. Rumors rumbled through the crew about what lay behind that door, but we respected Terion too much to push his boundaries.

What he did in his off hours was nobody's business but his. I'd be lying if I said I wasn't curious, though.

I might be the girl on Terion's arm at the party, but that was just a ruse. No one wanted to be the man on *my* arm. At least not after they learned I was broken. It was almost like my throbbing shoulder was a sign. *Pull yourself together, Mari. Stop moping about that bastard.* I moved my arm gingerly back and forth.

If we pulled off this heist, I'd lift the shadow of Terion's debt and prove my place. I'd stop feeling inferior. Maybe I'd belong at last. The captain, at least, had a little faith in me.

"Ever think you'd go to one of Dio's parties?" Zete asked, bumping shoulders with me.

My shoulder shrieked at the contact, but I only shot Zete a glare. He gazed innocently back. I sighed. "We threw lots of those back home."

Terion chuckled. I grew up in the swamps. No one threw lavish parties there. The closest we got was drinking home-made spirits and hoping no one would burn the house down when they got too drunk. And I wasn't even invited to that. I snuck in sometimes, though.

"This will be the one," Terion said, a familiar glint in his eye. He thought we'd succeed in every mission, seemingly forgetting every failure.

Terion was a lot of things—a feared sailor, a cocky pain in the ass—but I wanted this to go right for him. For us. "It will be," I agreed, with a grim smile.

He cocked a dark eyebrow. "That's a look I like." His suit gleamed in the sunlight.

"Good. It's a look that's going to get your father off your back."

His lips curved. "Even better. Suddenly I can't wait for this party."

Order Temptation and Tridents today!

# READ MORE BY ZORA FOX

Fae and Shadow duology
*End of the Forest*
*Trapped by the Fae*

Deathless Love series
*Wings and Blindness*
*Flowers and the Far Realm*
*Storm and Sanctuary*
*Flame and Warpaint*
*Full Moons and Vampires*
*Temptation and Tridents*
*Candle Wax and Sunlight*

Find all of Zora Fox's spicy fantasy romance titles on Amazon.